Published and distributed by:
Stenton Publishing
P.O. Box 17971
Memphis, TN 38187-7971
l.bronson@yahoo.com

Cover Concept: L. Bronson
Cover Design: L. Bronson
Editor: B. Littlepage

This book was printed, bound and distributed by:
Lightning Source Inc.
1246 Heil Quaker Blvd.
La Vergne, TN 37086
United States

Printed and copyrighted in the United States of America
10 9 8 7 6 5 4 3 2 1

ISBN: 978-0-9794268-1-0 51400

"...let's play?"

Dedication

For those who have been afflicted in a manner which has caused them to lose their innocence. To the ones in denial of this affliction, and for the ones who are unaware of how affliction can become a disease. The afflicted carry deep within them guilt, shame, embarrassment and are unable to share it for the purpose of healing and closure. This disease, passed on, forced onto them by people who misused the very nature of trust. Those scars of affliction are deep and require healing, which can take a lifetime.

How long do I have to endure this torture of mistrust?

Yes, I was naïve then, but the corruption has borne in me lust.

To think I never asked for this moment with you, to include me!

I was, well, in my innocence, breathing, living with respect of thee!

Now what am I to do? Knowing what you have done to me and made me do to you!

I can now never love or show that emotion I have for another…that part is no longer new.

You stole something that you can never give back!

My trust, my love, my respect, my joy, my happiness, sadness …internalized…fade…to black.

L. Bronson

Condition

"…let's play?"

I know it is getting late but I can't turn away from this scene on my computer. You should see it! The figures on the web pages are so enticing. They seem to welcome me into their world. As crazy as it sounds, I hear myself talking aloud to each image, it's weird. At other times I believe these pages have taken on some sort of emotional form where they are beckoning onto me to stay close to gaze upon its perceived beauty. The computer screen appears to understand and relieves me of the impression of being lonely. In this situation however, I am lonely. For some odd reason, I have come to believe that my current situation is my own imagination. Oh, how I would love to be there on the other side of this screen instead of here! But I don't ask myself what I would do once I am there. I'm partially afraid of the answer. However, I must bid farewell to the only entity that knows my every need. But wait, the screen calls me again and again to look further into the essence of being a provider for me. "Why do you provide me with such bliss?" I ask not looking for a response. Page after page, short video after short video, and the fulfillment never stops. This entity has held my attention for what…three hours now? Dammit! Even after I've reached the pinnacle of my release, it continues to call my name and I continue to answer. "Help me", I say from time to time to myself while I'm so vulnerable. My cry cannot be heard for I need something greater than my own presence. But alas, I must break free…right now or else I will become a prisoner again, if for another moment. Something within tells me that I could endure another moment. Man, how I love those moments! I am such a bad boy, yes I am! I'm a bad boy. I tell myself, "You bad…boy."

I make a quick break and start to shut down the computer system. As I wait for the system to close, I begin to cover up myself and hobble towards the bathroom. In my effort to cover up, I laugh at myself for attempting to cover up in a house that only includes me. In my mind, I justify this action as an act of habit.

Once in the hallway, I pause to listen for any noises and disturbances to my silence. Nothing. Believe it or not, this is my home and at this moment I feel like a stranger! My knees are a bit wobbly. I've made my way inside the bathroom, and begin to methodically clean up before considering what to do first on my "honey do" list for this Saturday.

I briefly recall what my wife wanted me to do today. I had become so distracted with my moment of pleasure. However, my wife gave me the task of finding a solution in rearranging the garage for more access. My wife has been complaining about the limited space between the parked cars and the shelves. To me, if she would park the car, leaving equal space on both sides of the vehicle then she would have access to both car doors.

But I think that if she were to lose a little size on that beautiful rump of hers, then she could get through the spaces. Who am I kidding? She isn't big at all! It (her rear) does look good on her. When she moves, it (her rear) moves to its own rhythm and each cheek moves with its own rhythm. It (her rear) has a beat within a beat within a beat when she walks about any space. I'm still trying to figure out how she keeps it so firm. It's like poetry in motion only with three simultaneous motions. To me, it doesn't matter what she wears, skirt, dress, jeans, period drawers, robe or coat. That thing (her rear) seems to call my name. This notion I truly believe. I try to respond to it every chance she lets me. Oh thank you for women!

Before I start the task, I finish washing; the temporary guilt of my previous endeavor fills my soul. The deepest parts of me cry shame, disrespecting of my own person and even childish behavior unbecoming of an adult. It's a weird presence as I occasionally gaze at myself in the mirror. I snicker slyly, knowing right now that I can't be caught.

To think here I am, thirty seven years of age, three children; one boy, and two girls, all about a year and a half apart and each one taking on teenage growth with vengeance! I have a beautiful wife, "my girl" as I call her, whom I met while on a break between college semesters in our junior year. During our time of courting, we fell off, only to return to one another. Man, the other encounters I had while I was away from her. Some were good, but many…well, I'm just glad I woke up in time. I know some of those situations with those other females were my fault and I hope that I didn't sustain any deep scars from them or on the contrary, I hope I didn't leave any of them in any type of emotional disarray. Anyway, I love my family, would give them the world if I could, I know that's not true, the world thing, but I believe that I would do everything in my power to keep them safe and secure.

I ignore the apparent factors that rule my inner being; I need help, always knew it, can't deny it and won't accept it because I've found reason to continue this predicament. At times my condition doesn't seem like a condition but like a disease which I have contacted from some other person. This infection as I like to think of it, keeps showing up within my body and the only way to control it, is to feed it. This is an infectious monster which has to be feed by its host with what it yearns as an emotional and physical entity; lust. This pleasure sensory should be used in the confines of marriage. Now isn't that a damn shame?

After washing, I take my wash cloth that I used for the purpose of containing my efforts of lust and run it through the running water, mixing it with soap to remove the evidence. I've found that hot water and soap have to be used repeatedly in order to remove the evidence. There again lies a sign from my efforts; this evidence is not to be tampered with, like in my case, it has strong physical characteristics. After which I ring out the wash cloth and place it on the side of the tub. I know my wife would not question the addition of a wash cloth because she would believe I just needed an additional one. But I press forward to put on my "work around the house" clothes, put on my old "sneaks" and head to the garage.

It's a little eerie, the feeling, of being alone in the house, which doesn't happen on a regular basis. However, this feeling parallels to my own inner feelings. I am alone in this encompassing emotion. It lays dormant ready to move to the surface in an instant. It doesn't take much to stimulate this emotion to appear within me. It could be a look from some unknown female, my own discovery of a physical endowment of any appealing female or just playing with innuendoes in a conversation that I shouldn't indulge in with fellow female workers or female friends. This disease that I have, I believe it to be one, keeps me separate from everyone else in my household and sometimes my surroundings. I cannot share this with another. So far, I have not shared this with my wife.

However, one similar to me who would have the same symptoms and urges would also stay separate from me. There would be no way that we could connect. Between the two of us we would probably know or have some idea of the other, but that would mean exposing ourselves in the interim. Because this emotion would no longer be my own, to cherish it, protect it, feed it, I would rather…just keep it to myself. But I know I have the will power to fight it, I just don't know where to start and I keep yearning to start over again after each experience. I tell myself that this time I going to start to deny the fulfillment that this emotion needs from me. But as I endure that long suffering of denying this need of my emotion, other stimuli that I did not pay attention to previously show up to push me over the edge. Hah, how can something external and inanimate push me over the edge? Or is it that I have suppressed this emotion in such a way as to build it up to a boiling point before each occurrence? Man, kicking this habit has been tough. I can truly relate my addiction to those addicted to drugs, and obsessions.

So, this is my dilemma and I hope by now you have a grasp of my prison. If you don't, then read on. I'm hoping that you can handle my story for it will not be pretty nor will it be dressed up nor will it end with the kind of ending you are so use to hearing about or even reading. This story is a tale of the possibilities that are within my grasp relating to my prison. This prison of mine has not only convicted me guilty, it has sentenced me to obtaining therapy…for the rest of my life or until such time that I can, in my opinion, demonstrate myself as a functioning person of society, whatever that is. While in society I have been given the authority and/or responsibility to contribute to the further proclamation of the existence of society. Now that part can be tricky if one of the ways I can contribute is... However, my conviction is no different than yours or anyone else; it's a hindrance that places upon its host a limit to everyday interaction with people and surroundings, a practiced mannerism.

You see, prisons are meant to contain, cause one to reflect internally about the wrong or right that was done against them or to come to terms with themselves and/or other people or even circumstances. But this same cage causes you to disconnect from the rest of the world using very primal instincts which tend to surface uncontrollably. As you become less of an integral part of society and your primal state of emotion and survival instincts take over, whatever is within your grasp at that time is what you hold on to as your reality.

This emotional conviction that I have is my own prison. I have built the cage to house this emotion. It doesn't matter if I inherited it or developed it to soothe the effects of some childhood torment or some manner in which to deal with life in general; I have it, can't get rid of it at the moment, and on most occasions, enjoy it. My prison allows me to move freely to stimulate it all day, some days when the moment dictates, such as being home alone. It is fortunate for me that I have not found a victim or a suitor to infect or to displace this emotion upon! My wife, for the most part, has held me in check with my prison so long as she stays within my grasp. I often wonder if she has been infected and doesn't know it. I could not bear to see another fall prey and become infected with my prison. Does it make sense? Sure it does, because as you read this I hope that you may want to question the very habit or habits that you have which keep you a prisoner. So every prisoner is in some strange way similar, if but faintly, in my opinion.

I've moved the car out onto the driveway path. As I get out of the car, I look around to see if any of the other neighbors are out this mid-morning. I lock the car and head toward the garage to move the other car. I was hoping I wouldn't have to face my next door neighbor of our adjoining twin home. My neighbor, if we met, would hold me to a long conversation and eventually would notice my discomfort in talking. I wouldn't want to offend him. But once inside the garage, I check around once more, panning to my left and to the right about the other twin homes.

So, I shut off the automatic garage door close to about three feet above the ground. "Where are my goggles?" To me that is a rhetorical question and I proceed to look for the eye protectors. After that, I turn on my music and begin my chore. All is well as I "jam" to some old school rap, symphony, rock, bebop jazz, a little country…what the hell, music. The chore or task that I have to complete isn't a hard one. Basically, all I have to do is rearrange the spaces in the garage, make it more useful. But if I rearrange the space of course I have to clean it. This is where the chore becomes an even longer one.

My day has return to normal, I am a functioning adult and no one cares so as long as I don't disrupt the normalcy of their day. But this day would be a different day. This day would throw me into a new frenzy. My emotion, my habit, my prison which I have kept in check for all of my life thus far would be tempted to cross over into the realm of possibility. I would be given a choice of the possibility to infect another, or giving to another a prison similar to the one which I now have built for myself. The thought of infecting another sickens me but a side of me ponders the thought…then I break again to my senses.

Eventually I would meet the one person who would send me over the edge…for good. I didn't know my wife would concede to having her, get this, her cousin's niece to stay with us for the rest of the summer. Does that make her a true relative to me? The stay will be about three and a half months. Now that is too long, but I didn't know this at the time. My wife wanted her niece, what is the title of this relative as it relates to me, to experience being around other life styles and out of the inner city living if not for a moment. Besides, my wife's niece's parents have been working at a feverish pitch to consolidate their life style...debt. But we haven't had my wife's cousin's family over to our house in a while. We usually make the visit when we visit my wife's uncle in the suburban section of the city.

Now I have been around my niece from time to time since the first day she came home from the hospital with her parents. I have aided in changing her diapers and helped with putting on her clothes as a baby. As she grew, I have cleaned her bruises, given her a spanking or two and have given her and her siblings a bath, one at a time or altogether. In many instances my children were mixed in the same bunch with my niece and her siblings as they bathed or were chastised. But as my niece grew I understood the separation when she, I heard from my wife, was now developing growth characteristics. At this point it wasn't growing hair, or physical development, but her perspective on being seen by her peers and especially an adult. I never argued nor wanted to venture into that realm; a growing young girl into a blossoming young woman at whatever level. I brushed off the condition because my niece's brother and my son were having the same trouble adjusting to that same development around the same time. These two had trouble being around me, another male!

My adjustment to my niece's development as well as her siblings and my children was easy. I would pay particular attention to compromising situations between them and myself. It was hilarious to see the uneasiness of my son, when, once he had to change in the same dressing room as me. I would just remind myself of the funny times leading up to the end of the bathing in the tub.

My niece, she's a doll and smart. However, because of her genuine love and affection for me in particular, or is this with all relatives, she tends to stay too close to me. I never noticed this behavior until her stay. Oftentimes I would humorously push her away or avoid her. My niece's father would laugh and reply. "...you know she just loves you to death!" Again statements like that would surface later and I almost didn't see it coming.

As I finish the rearranging of the shelving, I recall my first experience with what is my prison. I don't know why the thought would cross my mind now, maybe because I'm headed toward the garage door which leads into the kitchen, but the moment was too real. I began to walk blindly, with awareness of my every movement, robotic. I often suppress these memories by occupying my time with something other than what is on my mind. Better than that, I haven't had many instances where I've had to revisit these memories, but I often do by scraping just the surface of the memory.

I begin to recall my cousin and me cleaning the rectangular concrete backyard for my grandparents. My grandparents lived in the urban swell of the city in a row house, fifth house from the corner of an intersecting block at a time when people seemed to still care. The row home had four bedrooms that loomed huge at my age. There was a porch in the front which was under the front bedroom and steps leading from the porch to the sidewalk. The house contained a living room, a dining room, a kitchen and and a half bath which is called a backshed. This shed led to the backyard where my cousin and I were cleaning. Upstairs were the rooms and one large bathroom to accommodate all. In this house was a full length basement that extended from the end of the porch to the end of the backshed. In this space believe it or not there was another bath and sink enclosed for privacy.

It is summertime and for the two of us and our sisters, this is where we spent summers. His parents and my mother are off to work and we're here attending neighborhood summer camps part time, learning patience, reading, writing, forms of discipline and the genuine ability to tolerate one another respectfully. All of us occasionally stay overnight and sometimes for extended periods of time. My grandparents loved the company, we loved the company and it seemed their house was never empty with one group of us being there consistently.

The times I spent there were rewarding until another relative stayed this one summer. This relative, a young aunt visiting from my grandfather's side of the family would be my suitor. She was visiting from out west. She is very pretty and I remember telling my cousin that I wish I had a girlfriend that looked similar to her. My cousin laughed at my notion and explained to me that a thought like that was too far for an eight year old to understand. What did he know? We were young then and what do I really remember about that conversation?

During the cleaning in the yard, I had to use the bathroom and the only way to use the facility is to go through the ritual. I first informed my cousin that I had to go to the bathroom so as to not get in trouble when my grandparent(s) were looking for me. Then I move to enter the doorway into the house from the backyard. Ah, this is how the memory starts.

There in the doorway I had to remove my shoes and make certain that the door was closed behind me. After practicing all of this, I am now ready to head to the bathroom. In the meantime, I've begun my dance of deterring my release. It is getting even harder as I approach the bathroom. The anxiety has been building. But inside the bathroom I have to first wash my hands. Growing up I was constantly told that I could become venerable to some airborne disease if I didn't stay clean in my groin area. So as I wash my hands and dance the entire time until I finish the washing, my first release has come and gone. I pull my pants down to my ankles, trying not to disturb my underwear. I don't want to have to change pants. I look down at my underwear and notice the small stain of a light yellow color and how quickly it has spread over my underwear. It looks like a moving disease! For an instant it was fascinating of how liquids work but I can't bear the moment anymore and rush to pull my underwear down to my ankles. I rush to lift the toilet seat and as I point my appendage to start the flow of urine, in relief I indulge the moment by closing my eyes, leaning my head back slightly and allowing the flow to move through my body. If you've never experienced this…well, you'll figure it out…one day. As I finish, I flush the toilet with my elbow and again wash my hands because in my haste I have gotten some on parts of my hands. After washing my hands I check about the seat and around the floor because I know if I'm the one that is blamed for missing the seat…you should know how painful that beating will be to you. After performing the steps of how to be responsible in the bathroom I am left with the choice to either pull up my pants and risk the ridicule from my cousin later as a pants wetter or sneak upstairs and change my underwear. I took the latter and once upstairs I had to find a safe place to hang my soiled "undies" until later.

My entire world, my way of life changed from that point forward and even today I questioned what other choices I was left with on that day that would change the outcome. I first heard murmurs from the room that my aunt was occupying. This aunt was in her room with nothing on, lying back on the side of her bed and groaning, this I would later find out. So, as all curious children do, I peeked through the keyhole and silently watched until she was finished. I thought I was there for a long time but I would later deduce that I arrived at her climatic moment. When she rose, I had never seen what we children called at the time, a grown-up's body and the look of her body froze me. It was of a peculiar beauty, a figure that held my attention, yet alerted me that something was wrong with my opportunity to view this specimen of a curvaceous woman. I don't know why I didn't move at that moment because for some reason she came right to the door. I didn't panic because I was caught between looking and running. I figured I could run at the last minute. As we grow to understand why and how we were caught as children, I would realize how my aunt caught me that day. The shadows underneath the door and the occasional shuffling to stay comfortable were what gave away my presence. I was also breathing at an erratic pace. My aunt did not seem upset as she approached the door but I moved slowly when she opened the door. As I knelt still frozen with the fear of being caught, because I moved too late, on one knee, I looked up at her with widen eyes. She leaned over and whispered to me that she knew I was there and if I didn't come back on a particular day and time, she was going to tell on me. Then she looked about and told me to leave. Later, outside, my cousin teased me about not only having to go and urinate but I had to do a number "two". I denied his accusation but he wouldn't let up and eventually we got into a fight for which we were both punished simultaneously.

After I calmed down and my cousin and I became friends again, I began to think about my appointment and if I didn't meet it what would happen. I consulted my cousin on what he would do if he were in a similar situation and of course I lied about who was involved and the circumstances. During that time of discussion, I often wondered what was really coming out of my mouth back then. I was too young to know what to say or remember. In addition, there has been too much time in between my many present moments and that incident in my past.

Later that evening after dinner, my cousin, our sisters and I made ourselves comfortable in the living room on the floor to watch television. My aunt joined us and participated in our discussion of the boring show on television that our grandparents made us watch. We were told by my aunt to tone down our talking and to not laugh so loud before the patience of our grandparents reached their limit. Obliging her instruction, she eventually rose, but before she departed, she made more small conversation with all of us and looked at me with a stare, slightly nodding her head with the understanding that the time was near for me to perform my duty. She left the area and I waited and waited some more. I became afraid of what might occur and if I was really in trouble. As with most kids who often stayed in trouble, I could be certain that trouble was somewhere close to me. My cousin began to tease me about not responding to his many questions regarding the show on television that for the life of me I still can't remember. Eventually I rose and slowly moved out of the living room when my grandmother stopped me to inquire where I was headed. As usual I explained that I was headed to the bathroom. However, grandmother explained that there was more than one bathroom to use other than the one upstairs. I countered that I didn't want anyone to see me in the bathroom. Her response was that I didn't have enough to show and that I could not possibly produce that bad of a smell at my age. She looked in the direction of my grandfather for understanding and he just shrugged his shoulders. I defended myself and she laughed at me with a hand wave of conceding to my wish.

My walk upstairs was one of the longest journeys that I could remember at that age. As I ascended the steps, I glanced back hoping someone would call my name or that an incident would occur that would beckon my attention. However, nothing came to my assistance and I continued up the stairs. When I arrived at the door, I stood there again hoping for some miracle but then my aunt spoke from the other side asking if it was me standing there. I replied and she told me to open the door.

Inside, she lay under the covers as if she didn't want me to notice anything about her. I could still remember how she looked hours ago. I laughed to myself about how childish she looked. It resembled my sister or my female cousins when my cousin and I would pull the covers off of them to give them a chill. My aunt instructed me to get undress. Undress in front of you at my age? I pleaded with her not to have me do that. I knew the beating was about to commence. I could feel the "whelps" from the lashes of the belt. My skin crawled with the expectations of the consistent pain. She explained to me that if I didn't then she was going to beat me first and then tell on me. So I turned my back to her and proceeded to remove ALL of my clothes. First, I removed my sneakers, then my pants and socks and so on. I didn't want to turn around to allow her to see my little glory. She snickered, explained that I had a cute set of buttocks and I became frustrated at her laughing. My aunt then told me to get into bed. So I slid into bed backwards, again to hide my boyhood, my pride. I entered from the right side of the room into the bed opposite of her side.

Under the covers it was very warm and I could smell a familiar smell or at least that is what I could relate to the smell. Tomatoes! It smelled liked tomatoes! Funny, but that's what it smelled like to me. To this day, I recall that odor from other females of previous relationships. On the other hand, I enjoy eating tomatoes in almost any form. I laid there silent and unsure what to expect next. My aunt also continued to just lie there motionless in bed. I expected something weird to occur, but nothing happened for what seemed several minutes. I glanced over at my aunt and she slowly turned her head to look at me. Her smile seemed so pleasant, innocent and caring. It was the first time that I could see some gentleness in her eyes. Most of the time she gave me a glaring stare. But that moment assured me that I wasn't going to get a beating, but I was still nervous as to why I would be in bed with my aunt with no clothes on my body. Eventually my aunt slowly reached over with her hand from her left side and began to caress my boyhood. Her touch alarmed me at first; I didn't want to look down. Then it tickled and then…something felt weird. I mean, I liked the feeling, but something was weird. I looked over to my aunt who had by now closed her eyes as she continued to caress me. I started to speak out to say that I didn't want to do this anymore. But as I started to speak, she leaned over and gently kissed me with her eyes closed! I had my mouth opened a bit in shock and then she stuck her tongue in my mouth. Whatever she had earlier, I knew it contained something strawberry and sweet. As I held my eyes opened, I intermittently tasted the strawberry and she became a little more aggressive in her kissing. I wanted her to stop, so I began to pull away slowly. She moved closer and shoved her left hand under my head to pull or hold me in place as she continued to kiss me. Well, the strawberry taste was wearing off and I was getting tired of kissing. She kissed me so long that I had never felt my jaws become numb. Before I could embrace the numbing in my mouth, my aunt rolled over on top of me! Her movement was a smooth, calculated and an experienced one. I didn't feel her weight over me. But she loomed large and intimidating. As I started to squirm about to be freed, my aunt began to dance seductively, rubbing her hands around her breasts. I paused to look closely at her breasts. She possessed nice round aureoles and perky nipples, like those of a baby's bottle. I was mesmerized and watched as she moved about. My aunt leaned over me bracing herself with her hands and leaned down to kiss me again. I had grown weary of this action, and turned my head again, only to have my aunt turn me to face her. She reached out and held my hands with her hands, and slid her body up over my boyhood. "Whatever it was", this is what I said to myself at that time, it felt slippery, wet, moist, and oh yes, warm. For some odd reason, I wanted to feel more, but then something told me that something was wrong. This feeling began to emerge with great force within me and I wanted to find relief. I squirmed, and my aunt tightened her hold on me.

Now she pressed down on me, moving about as if she was seeking something with her body and didn't want to look for it. Then I felt it! It was an intense shock and it correlated with my other feeling of fleeing the scene. I recall hearing something of a serenity type song. I lay in purgatory to what was taking place and my aunt took full advantage. She methodically bounced on me and rolled her body as if she was playing with a "hoola-hoop". I became fascinated by her self enjoyment. I had almost forgotten about my own ill feelings and suspected that she would stop soon. This act of hers was a mystery to me at that moment. I felt a good feeling, but this was not where I wanted to stay. But I didn't know how to remove her.

I deduced long before I entered the room that if I made any noise, it would be my fault! It would be my fault for being in the room, my fault for lying to my grandmother and my lists of guilt feelings was a long one. Eventually, I slipped away from my own feelings and became more methodical in my actions. I drew no more attention from my aunt and I didn't respond to her. As I became more relaxed and relieved, I would later find out; I had slipped out. By that time she was finished with me anyway and rolled off of me, I immediately peeked under the covers and I was very shiny in my pelvic area. There was still an alert response from my boyhood. It looked as if I had spilled some clear melting jelly on myself.

When my aunt moved, I dropped the covers and tried to look innocent. The covers pressed firmly against my boyhood and I could feel the jelly-like covering adhering to the sheets. She

reached over and pulled me close for another kiss. Instead she
kissed me about my face and body and whispered in my ear that
this was our little secret and that I should, no, couldn't tell anyone,
ever. Defeated, I looked at her with questioning eyes and she
reminded me of when I peeked at her and that she would tell only
if she had to tell. She explained that she would only do that if I
broke our trust. I agreed out of fear and she grabbed my hands and
moved them over her breasts. She asked me if I liked how they
felt. This time I felt the two big eyes and there were little pimples
over most of the area. They felt as if they contained some sort of
fluid similar to nice sized water balloons. I acknowledged with a
nod or tow and looked again at her with questions. My aunt
moved away and told me not to get up or move, so I did. She got
up, put on a robe, and walked out of the room. I laid there in
bewilderment, not knowing how to understand what just happen or
what was to happen next. My mind began to spin and I felt
"quezzy". About the same time, my aunt returned with a soapy
wash cloth and began to clean me. I watched remembering when I
was younger how my mother would wash me, but this time my
head kept spinning. When my aunt returned again, she helped me
dress and when she finished, she hugged me and thanked me and
explained that from time to time she would need me to help her
with this matter. I started to ask her what this matter is called. She
placed a hand over my mouth and whispered in my ear that the key
word to know when we would do this again was, "Do you want to
play?" I tried to snatch away from her hold, astonished at her line
that would conjure up this moment again. She pulled me closer
and hugged me again and explained that every now and then this
happens to a female who is about her age and that she had to find
someone she could trust to help her. She looked down at me with
those trusting eyes and asked me if I trusted her and would I help
her again. I said nothing but she again hugged me and sent me on
my way. Before I left her room, she explained to me to tell my
grandmother that she wanted to ask me some questions about
going to the park. My eyes widened because my cousins, my
sisters and I could only go to the park on occasion and I could

count the times. So off I went with a made up half smile of the entire moment. My mind was empty and all I could do was replay the moment or moments.

I entered the living room and my grandmother looked over to me with a snicker, asking me if I got rid of all of it. I looked at her confused and then realized what she meant. I kinda laughed back and my grandmother noticed the embarrassment. She started to inquire why I had taken so long and I remembered what my aunt had told me to say. My grandfather called me over to take a long look at me to satisfy his curiosity. He asked me was I feeling okay and I reply yes. He looked over at my grandmother and she looked and I straightened up to explain that I was a little tired. Again my grandfather looked over toward my grandmother with no response. She said nothing more and I took my place on the floor replaying the moment or moments over and over again with my aunt. None of my cousins or my sister inquired about my whereabouts and continued in their interest of the show playing on the television.

Amazingly, I don't recall my cousin asking me any questions that night about my using the bathroom, nor did we indulge in any other conversations. The last thing I remember about that moment was awaking the next day with a slight headache at one end of the bed with my cousin at the other. My cousin was sneaking up to me to play with me by slightly touching my ears or eyes until I finally awoke. When I did, he told me that it was Saturday morning and he wanted to rush downstairs to turn on the television first before our sisters. This way we could watch all the shows we liked.

Situation

It has been about two weeks now and my niece has finally settled into her room and the house. My children, rather my girls were a bit envious at first that she was the only kid in the house with her own room besides my son. They would all congregate in the room given to my niece, discussing teenage things, whatever is the new thing and constantly trying to exclude my son. But they all seemed to get along fairly well. Their moments were going along so well that my wife thought it would be nice for all of us to go out as a family. My wife decided miniature golf would something that wouldn't offend anyone and not as challenging. She thought that now that her niece was settled in that she should start experiencing how we do things as a family. Fine!

We informed them all of our decision to have a family outing and I explained that the best thing to wear on this outing was pants. I wasn't too sure about the bugs since we might be out into the evening. As usual the girls complained and my son was dressed and ready. As usual my wife had to examine him to assure herself that he was presentable to the public. He passed and I waited with him in the living room while we both waited for the females. My son asked me was all women like this, in needing more time for any and everything. I explained to him to get use to it, don't ask that question and learn patience. I also explained to him that there are moments in a man's life that he should learn how to adjust and relax because there can sometimes be humor in the smallest effort that is made.

All of them came downstairs together, my wife in the rear and looking like an older sister. There is just something about how jeans fit a woman! She looked good and casual by my standards except she had on dress shoes. I spent the next fifteen minutes explaining and convincing my wife and the girls that we would be standing and walking a great deal before sitting down. I went on to say that shoes without any cushioned support will aggravate your back or knees. That's when I noticed that my girls had on similar outfits. They all looked at me as if I had committed the worst offense and slowly moved back upstairs, whispering as they went. By now my son was snacking and watching some sports channel. I could not resist and joined him. At that moment I felt like we were brothers waiting on our mother, but I never told him this thought. I was beginning to worry about them because I started to become comfortable watching TV.

Now this time when they all came downstairs, my wife had changed her jeans into some khaki styled Capri pants that came to her calves in length. She has some big legs! I mean nice size calves and thighs. My girls followed the same dress code as well as well my niece. But there was something different about my niece. Her style of dress allowed her "attitude" to show some. Her movements were more of seduction. I hoped that she didn't notice the amazement on my face. My niece caught my expression which was the last thing I wanted her to know. I looked away and never looked back into her direction for awhile. I thought quickly that somehow I was going to pay for that look.

We began to move toward the door when my niece came over to thank me for allowing her to come and stay for the summer. In saying this, her gesture was to come over and hug me, and bury her face into my chest. She squeezed me hard and made her rear protrude out. Because I'm taller than she, I'm 6ft. 4 ins. and she is all but 5ft., I could look over her back and see this gesture in full bloom. From my vantage point, I could see over her backside down to the top of her pants…I gathered myself and tried not to look at anymore than that. I explained to her that she is part of the family as a way of deflecting her intentions. Now my wife, looking on, smiled at her niece's gesture and my acceptance. For a moment, my prison tapped me on the shoulder and I ignored it.

The miniature golf game had brought us together. I parked the car trying to find a marker for when we returned. The miniature golf place had several levels from novice on up to pro. I'm not sure what is a pro miniature golfer. But if you can made a living at the skilled activity, I would consider taking it on as a job. This was something that we hadn't done in awhile as a family but it seemed like old times, but on a different level. We argued, teased and laughed at one another but nothing had become too serious. My prison was somewhere enjoying something else on its own. However, it was around the ninth hole when my prison would tap me again on my shoulder. I believe it became bored.

Here is where my niece was to take her shot after my two daughters. She needed to make a difficult shot. This was a shot that everyone had trouble maneuvering through. When you started at the tee, the only thing you could see was the flag in the hole. In between the hole and the tee was a wall which rose and fell at different angles as a panoramic wall. But beyond the wall there were many other peaks and valleys of the green which set in between many of the walls. We all made it through with some difficulty. However, since we were keeping score, my niece was falling further behind and becoming a bit discouraged about the game. The further behind she fell, the more discouraged she became at continuing to play. My wife in her empathetic wisdom coaxed me to assist my niece. I arose reluctantly from the walls surrounding the course to try to help her as my wife looked on with admiration.

If my niece could maneuver on her first shot then she could maybe gain a little ground on her score. I demonstrated to my niece first and encouraged her to take a try at the stance first before actually taking her shot. She showed apprehension in practicing the same stance and taking the shot. I could hear my daughters whispering concern about my niece's ability to make this shot. My son just watched ready to laugh at a moment's notice. My wife, however now joined me in assisting our niece. She stopped near our niece and explained that she thinks she has the correct posture to make the shot, but could I help her one more time. I didn't know what that meant until it was too late. My wife explained to me to go over again and stand with her! To my dismay, I walked over to my niece and stood behind her, wrapping my arms around her to hold the golf club with her. As I explained, she slowly moved back and almost pressed up against me. I, anticipating this action and the reaction of my condition could not allow anyone else to notice. So I continued to demonstrate to her the technique and tried to ignore the loud tapping on my shoulder from my prison. She questioned me about her swing and I assured her that she had gotten the technique. As I finally moved away and watched from almost behind her, she took her swing with success. Everyone cheered for her and I cheered also, but my eyes were moving over the rear of her body, now why did I do that?

I hadn't paid much attention until now that her khakis were of the low riding type or that she was more endowed than what I believe she possessed. She also had on the wrong color underwear, rather thong. Colored stripes under a light tan were not the type of colors to blend together. As she jumped and my family came over to cheer her on, she looked over to me and thanked me with a smile.

That smile she gave me was more of a thank you in a seductive display. Right then I started to convince myself that she is only exploring the effects of her movements on holding/getting a male's attention and that she was not taught the proper way at her age to demonstrate such actions. Or was I imagining all of this and not looking at what was actually occurring. At that moment I don't recall.

At the fourteenth hole, again my niece explained her difficulty and the need to stay within a respectable distance from my kids. Again my wife urged me to assist her and again we assumed a similar stance. However, this time my niece decided to take a chance and tempt fate. As she began her swing, she backed up just a little more and came out of her swing awkwardly. In the meantime, she had conjured my prison by leaning back too long and I allowed her to feel just enough of me, while I held her, she looked up in disbelief. I felt so perverted yet I wanted to alert her that my prison was at the edge of being released into its full form. The moment was quick enough not to alert my wife who came over to assist the two of us to stand properly. Neither my niece nor I would make any eye contact again until the seventeenth hole. I was embarrassed and yet I wanted to explore a possibility that made me feel filthy. Instead I became focused on the game and the task at hand. During the rest of the play, I was thankful but yet slightly disappointed that my niece was able to hold her position in the scoring. This would mean less interaction and there was little reason for anyone to be concerned anymore. We chatted, laughed and played until the end. It was apparent that some of the luster of the game had come to an end and everyone seemed to just play up until that moment. In the meantime I would cause my prison pain and lock it down for the rest of the family gathering. We walked through the parking lot laughing and trying to figure where to eat. My wife and I decided on something close which was the pizza place across the street.

We made our way through the crowds that stood near the counter where we were trying to order. Finally we got our turn to order and looked about for seating near the rear. There were people shuffling in out as we found our seats next to the corner table. We sat at the picnic styled seating and that was when my wife wanted to subtly thank me for encouraging every one during this gathering. She sat close to me while we ate at the diner. No one was sitting at the table next to the window. However, none of the kids wanted to sit with us or next to us. I believed our demeanor would've rub off on them. Besides they chatted up a storm and kept moving about. s owe told them to at least get a table close enough so that we could keep an eye on them.

So after getting some items to eat, my wife and I sat down again to rest. I could see that she was relieved that our suggestion went well for the family and it got everyone to act normal around our niece. But my wife wanted to thank me more in an affectionate manner. So my wife started to touch my knee and move her hand up my leg in increments and then remove her hand. She was good at increasing the length of her movement, then retracting it again to start over. I prayed she didn't go as far as I wanted her to go with me. I tried to look inconspicuous as she continued playfully. Her intermittent yet continuous movements enticed me so that I wanted to just get up and run. What made matters worse was that my niece was now on the other side of the table across from me and must have taken notice. She seemed to have been taking a break from all the talk and horse play she and my kids were doing. Damn she knows too much too soon. I felt

~ 21 ~

uncomfortable with my wife's increasing gestures and then I wanted my niece to catch a glimpse of what could happen with us. It never happened and again I felt filthy in thinking of such gestures.

The similarities to this event were uncanny. This was how my aunt played with me one day at the kitchen table during breakfast. Again, my moments came and went and sometimes I just suppressed them. At other times the moments all meshed together in a lapse which made me dwell on them longer to decipher the extent and how it related to me in my growth. But this one had grown within me as did some of the others of my past.

I believed if my wife did not continue her appreciative efforts, the dream state would've past and I would've been relieved of controlling my prison. Instead my darling wife, unknowing to her soothed my tension and the moment came in brief stages. I was able to stay alert to the present actions and conditions concerning all who was around me while dwelling on my moment. It seemed to last longer than I thought!

But I could see in my state of mind that my cousin was on my right side and my aunt was on the other and I seemed to ignore everything she did. I tried to alert him indirectly, but I guess at that age you were not supposed to know those signs. After my aunt sat down next to me she looked at me to prepare me for what she was about to do. I looked back at her with a questionable look just before I could surmise what was possible between us. After several minutes had past and everyone else at the table was comfortable eating and talking, my aunt reached between my legs and positioned my boyhood into a position which would cause my boyhood to be looking up directly at me through my underwear! This is my adult psyche speaking from a boy's perspective. Again I can't recall the appearance of my appendage. But what was also strange to me now as an adult was how I could show the protrusion of my boyhood if I had on underwear briefs? As I look back on that moment, I have been thinking over and over of how my boyhood looked up at me imploring my means of rescuing it from the clutches of...the thought always end there.

My cousin and I had gotten into the kitchen before our sisters and sat at what we considered the prime seats; close to the refrigerator. From there my aunt would round the table asking each of us who wanted what type of cereal and continued until she reached the last, me. She sat next to me so that she could orchestrate the further distribution of cereal and milk.

As we all sat bickering, sometimes yelling, joking and laughing, no one paid attention to my aunt rubbing between my legs. She just took a seat and without hesitation went to work on me! I fidgeted in my seat displaying my discomfort, but she continued. As this moment continued, it was difficult to eat my cereal without a pause between each taste. It looked as if I was trying to savor mine to be the last in order to tease everyone else. Finally she paused and got up to make another round for everyone and I tried to finish my cereal before she had gotten to me. As she made her rounds I thought I saw her bring her hand up to her face to smell. I'm not even sure about this part and maybe I'm just filling in the gaps of my story. Nonetheless, I hoped that I could finish and maybe leave but I was hungry and wanted to request more cereal and milk. This I thought would give me more time to figure out what to do next. I thought I could delay her enough until I could finish my last bowl and leave. Who was I kidding at my age? But I felt to this day that this was my intent.

As my aunt sat back down she slowly started to move into action. That's when my grandmother came into the kitchen and began giving orders for our daily choirs. Once she finished that, she yelled at me for being too close to my aunt and sent my aunt to her room to put on more clothes underneath her housecoat. Rather, she had to put on a t-shirt or a bra, probably another color of panties or even pants. This part of the story never dawned on me until later in life when I saw a neighbor dressed in the same manner. I saw even more on my neighbor then I did on my aunt.

After my aunt left the kitchen, I became the butt of ridicule from the rest of the group. They teased me for attempting to play on our aunt's sympathy for more cereal. Or better yet, that I demonstrated female tendencies which could made me seem less of male. I had no way to explain that our aunt was the cause and I was too afraid to tell the truth. If I did tell the truth at that moment we would have to wait for another adult to come in to pour the cereal and milk. The adults were more apt at cheating us in our portions.

The thoughts, feelings and emotions were brief. No one noticed and I didn't want any of the kids to see my discomfort in my seat but my wife took notice and became offended. I tried to explain to her that this was not a good moment with the kids in such an excited mood; anything could happen in an instant with them around. One of the kids could get up and attempt to sit with us and their discovery would not be pleasant. Eventually, she understood, after my several explanations and apologies.

I thought all was well and soon thereafter, we were headed to the car. When we arrived at the car, the kids were trying to figure out who wanted which seat. Here my niece tested the waters again with me. She moved in between my two daughters and quickly asked me for assistance. Instead my son tried to offer, but she argued with him and he retaliated. I moved in between them and asked her what she wanted. Her request was simple; how could all of them fit in the back seats with only enough seat belts for three. Good question. I explained that she would have to share the seatbelt near the door on either side. She agreed and bent over first in order to slide across the seats. As I gazed at her posterior, my wife quickly interrupted the move of our niece and instructed her to sit down like a lady and shift herself with her bottom into a position next to my oldest daughter. She showed disappointment but made the move slowly in order to give me the last glimpse of her bottom. My wife's voice was slow rising and she explained to our niece that she should quicken her movements. I looked over to my wife and all she did was roll her eyes with her sigh.

Back home in the privacy of our room, my wife and I

debated, discussed and evaluated our niece's actions at the car. I tried to defend her because I felt guilty that she was caught in the act by my wife. But my wife expressed another point of view that I identified with; our niece's ability to allure. My wife expressed great concern over where she obtained such a sense and was she the only one expressing this type of attitude. Then it hit me that she was implying about our girls. I couldn't argue with her about it because I wasn't a female and besides this type of behavior was what attracted males to females. It was how much of the display that at female should leave out for a male's imagination that left her concerned. She was trying to explain in few words and in a manner of respect that our niece was trying to give away all of her ability to allure at a first glance. My wife tried to figure out from past experiences at what time did our niece start to demonstrate this kind of behavior. She was even more concerned that if our daughters hadn't already picked up on our niece's behavior then they too had developed that type of mentality on their own. They're all in the same age bracket; early teens. My wife began to curse herself for not being a better mother to our girls. I was overwhelmed for a moment as to how many different angles of assessment had developed from our niece's bending over at the car.

Eventually my wife had calmed down and we together decided how we were going to monitor our niece's behavior in a manner that would not alarm the other kids nor embarrass her at any time. We would also pay more attention to our daughters to see how much they either picked up or had already developed and was looking for ways to demonstrate away from us. This would be a task I was not ready for nor wanted to handle. It pained me to know that my daughters had the ability to do those things which I was accustomed to seeking out in other females for pleasure.

As we concluded the course of action I began hinting to my wife about what she mentioned to me earlier in the evening. I have to hand it to her for trying, I didn't fully appreciate her effort, but it was no use at that time. She explained she was a bit drained from expressing all of those wandering thoughts over our niece. She had been holding on to them since the incident and trying to stay focused on other matters. We eventually prepared for bed.

In bed however, I tried again and this time my attempt was met with a slow increasing argument. For the next twenty or so-minutes, my wife and I argued about having this intimate moment and how my advances offended her. I tried to explain the rubbing at the put-put course, what she had on for the event, how she took off her clothes in preparation for bed, what she had on underneath because I wasn't upstairs when she was getting dressed, I tried to cover every moment. It ended with neither one of us being able to wish the other a good night with respect and placing space between each of us as we lay in bed. My wife swore that this encounter was something I had prepared earlier in order to convince her to have an intimate moment. I wasn't sure that she was convinced of the matter and I pursued. Eventually I gave, no, we gave into the spell that was beginning to take hold of one of us, sleep. I laid there unable to sleep, unable to log onto the computer for gratification, scared to take advantage of my wife as she slept and scared to perform those personal duties in bed while she lay next to me and then catching me in the act. Now that would be embarrassing.

My mind wandered, this caused me to become restless and when I eventually started to sleep, I was laying halfway on my stomach. The position I was in didn't feel comfortable and as I tried to relax I found myself finding comfort by draping one leg over the upper portion of my wife's thighs. I quickly realized my position and then noticed that my left hand was now draped across my wife's rear. Her rear felt good to the touch and I gently squeezed periodically until I succumbed again to the sleep.

My mind wandered to another moment, a moment when my care and affection for my wife was young. We had gone on an outing of one of her friends. I believe it was a family reunion or something for her friend; my dream is now being corrected. I try to concentrate on my wife and I, and not the circumstances of the event in my dream. The choice I made about the event is that there is a family reunion. My wife and I have been enjoying the festivities and had no problem interacting with people hopefully we might see again. At moments, her friend and she are talking with other females and I am left alone to try to mingle with the other males I think are close to my age. A stroke of luck would give me the chance because males can bond around sports and I was welcomed in with caution.

My wife, rather my girl, at the time, is beautiful in some type of material shorts and a matching shirt with short sleeves. Her hair is braided starting from the center of the front of her head and wraps around one side towards the back. There, her hair is braided into a pony tail resting between the middle of her shoulders. She is happy and we're not old enough to drink legally but the effects of a little drinking have showed in our mannerisms.

After playing some "guys against the girls" type of games, we'd become a bit tired as did many of the other people. It was just our luck that I had a blanket rolled up in the trunk of my car and rush, well walked briskly, but in my mind I'm rushing, to retrieve it. We found a space away from all the games in a low grassy space next to a small embankment over looking a wide river. The only thing that I could remember was my wife pressed up against me and my draping my arm over her waist. The next morning we were awakened by some of the younger kids who were also in attendance. They stood afar off some, talking amongst themselves, waiting for one of us to react. They eventually became bored and disappeared. When I rose, it became apparent that my wife and I had given them the impression that we were trying to have sex. As she sat up next to me, we realized that my manhood was pressing against my khaki pants and that my wife held my hand inside the front of her pants!

As I laughed in my sleep about the dream, reality struck me in the form of being in an identical position with my wife as she slept. Everything was the same except my excitement. I wanted my wife so bad and I tried to devise ways to persuade her from her sleep to indulge with me. It took many kisses and kisses in many places in order to get a response of a minute form. I thought she was being coy with me, but then I realized that she was actually asleep. As I tried other means to excite her, I again, thought that she persisted in not responding to my advances. I eventually rolled away from her in disgust. Frustration was overtaken by the sleep that I was deprived of earlier and it took me quickly.

In the morning, my wife asked me did I try anything with her. I denied her allegations. She explained how she could not stay comfortably asleep and thought it was something more. I admitted to her in part, hoping I would not have to explain in detail. But I assured her that we did not indulge ourselves and that I had more respect for her than what she was giving me. After she was satisfied with what didn't occur, we continued our day with me continuing my displeasure with her not indulging me.

Agitation

In the last few days my prison has indicated to me its desire for some release. Actually it has only been three days to be exact. The slightest gesture by someone generates a hint that at any moment, my prison will be knocking at its doors. To give you an example, a brush of the body from my wife or a compromising touch from a female friend, or engaging in a discussion on a subject which contains sexual innuendoes by a fellow female colleague. I know this sounds perverted, but this is how much I want to stop my own willingness to release my prison. Often times my wife acknowledges how much excitement she can cause within me. She explains that at least she knows I'm excited for her. But at other times she wishes I could have better control or rather that I have not matured enough in the category of self restraint when we begin to indulge ourselves in our moment.

Personally, I've been avoiding many encounters with my niece and I am now aware that she is aware and that we both can see the awareness in each other. It scares me to think that with each encounter there is a perception and anticipation for what the next moment will bring with her. Again, all of this seems surreal, or is it just my own private "Idaho" of beliefs? I dare not tell nor ask, but there is some guilt that I feel about how she interacts with me now. I hope I didn't conjure up that demon within her that lies dormant and possibly would've stayed dormant if it not for my undoing. Or that I've tempt her into welcoming a side that externally waited for her call and then to inhabit her with a drive of desire that she could not understand. Or on the other hand, I encourage her to release the demon that dwells within her that she doesn't understand how to control it or to keep in check. I pray she doesn't become my victim. Her undoing would be something I could not live with, it's no different than having one of my children falling victim.

But I've pressed on to avoid facing those conditions and situations with my niece, because at the moment, I can't allow her to help me, my wife can only help me, no, come to my aid, on occasion. I need this aide because I don't want to establish a partner of outside dimensions. However, it would be very hard to digest the fact that a new host in my own house could in turn re-infect me with my own disease. This is why I need a host/partner outside of my home where they too would be left to deal with this disease/prison on their own. I know this is not the answer, but my prison grows and yearns to be fed. To involve myself in this matter would be callous of me and I know, no, I believe I have that type of capability, to go forth with this type of decision. However, I still hope to have a conscience of some sort which would help to stop me from further pursuing this matter. The thought of someone totally external and detached enlightens me and I try to figure out the "how".

But having a new partner would mean engaging in dialogue, then finding out how much that person would be interested in just being a physical partner and then finally proposing this arrangement, hoping that she won't back out. That would be tough and long and right now I don't have the patience nor could I go that far against my wife. I believe I still have some morals that are part of my demeanor. But the lines sometimes become dashed, skewed, and vague when I entertain these thoughts. This type of thinking could go on and on if I don't break free of my own spell.

But, I must find relief! I debate with myself about going to a strip club just to be allowed to wet my underwear after a lap dance. That is really not any fun. To think, I would have to find something to hold my release, then dispose of it. I believe that would bring about embarrassment if I was discovered with the evidence or in a compromising position which would give that impression. Only places I would like to visit are more of the non-upscale type where you can get fulfillment quickly and cheaply. The unfortunate side is that you would need to take a friend with you for safety reasons. That is not the only reason why I don't want to visit, I know within myself, deep down, if I was given an unadulterated moment, I'm not sure to what extent that I could resist the temptation. Besides the thought of succumbing to some non threatening disease which I would have to explain how I was infected with it. Or better yet developing into a stalker because I believe this particular female is the one whom I could indulge myself with and infect without regard.

I've also entertained the thought of going to a bookstore and picking up a very detailed and lengthy magazine. I could peruse the listings freely and pick out the one that gave me the most motivation. However, I would have to venture way out of the city limits just to find a store or go to one that is in some bad shape as in the case of being a building that was designed to accommodate secrecy. Again, I just can't go to any place for the fear of being seen by someone who would eventually talk to my wife in some manner. All I need is for something like that to get out and having to explain this to my wife, how embarrassing.

As another alternative, I thought about renting a movie or better yet borrowing one from one of my friends. I would have to revisit a store where I had membership some time ago and then renew for a fee. It would be difficult to find the one that contained the details I was looking for and with some length. Another way would be to just go to a rental place that contained those types of films for rental and then I would have to apply for membership. Again, this could take some time or I would have to show up at home with the movie and then wait for the right moment to view it. On the other hand, borrowing one from a friend meant striking up a conversation only to be asked when I would visit again with my wife. Then I'd have to go over to this person's house, strike up another intriguing conversation with his wife, stay a bit, look through his private collection when the opportunity permitted and stay awhile longer before leaving. Now we all know that this friend's wife would ask about my "out of the blue" visit, and this friend would have to explain, or, again, this friend's wife would eventually speak to my wife and systematically introduce my visit into their conversation. Man this just doesn't get easy.

So instead I have been going through my daily routines of work, fatherhood and husbandry trying to maintain my composure about my prison's release. I've had to stay focused to remind myself with every encounter not to frown nor seem fidgeting when in the presence of others. I also have to be aware no to come across as being too happy or gleeful, this too would raise some suspicions.

At work it was easy because I spent time outside of the department inspecting our finished work. I could be out from the time I enter the office, getting plans, surveying equipment and GPS units in order to establish marks and points. Often I'm occupanied by another male, a coworker and throughout the day I'm distracted with work or conversation. However, if there is an encounter which stimulates the rise of my prison, my coworker would indirectly aid me in countering the effects. He doesn't know how he is protecting me from myself.

At home, after work, my son and I would throw football passes to on another to pass time. I'd have him run routes and hit him with some accuracy, but he was better at passing to me. On other occasions if we weren't playing some other sport, I'd show him how to drive the car or just talk man talk. This was when I was torn a bit with passing along my prison as an inheritance to my son and watching it grow within him as a seed. At that moment I'd hope he would be better at performance, suppression and hiding the prison. But I could never pass along this prison to him. I was glad when I spent this time with him, because it was at these moments that encouraged me to seek help.

On other occasions I awkwardly spent time with my daughters, discussing fashion, boys, if they'd allow me and where to shop. But as I carried on conversations with my daughters I discovered how precious and pure innocence was to children. With that I realize how attractive it could be to those who preyed or wanted to feed on that purity. But my girls made me feel as if I was their protector, the one who would prevent my prison from encapsulating them as I am now. I wish they would stay in their presence state.

As for my wife, man we would play on words with one another, all innuendos. Other times we would just tease each other to no end. Our conversations were so in depth that we would research the subject, preparing to pick up the conversation on another occasion. She is my girl, the one who makes me feel like I never get old. The one who helps me see more good in the world than the world would allow to be seen. I liked the way we just "talk".

However, neither of these fulfilling parts of my life could embrace my desire to feed my prison. This has caused me such pain to the extent that I have been engaging in precise arguments with my wife for no other reason than to gain her attention. My slow moving upheaval of emotion has not moved her to inquire of my pain and the cause. Instead, she endures moment after moment with soothing words of encouragement. She makes me sick! Not literally. Of all times to become a loving, caring and understanding mate, she picks each encounter with me and quickly diffuses my yearning to have my desire. It makes me feel childish, but I pursue the completion of this so-called need to the end. Hopefully she will bend. So I lay in wait for a moment when the reciprocal will occur whereby she is now expressing some emotion related to a troubling subject and needs care and attention.

Lately though, she has been ignoring me a little more and I blame the time of the month. I can't be sure of that, but I equate her mood to that since we have tapered off our moments of persuasive conversation and indulgence. I've inquired indirectly but she has not responded with her explanation of not feeling well. I don't want to appear to be begging like I'm on drugs or something to my wife.

Other times I want to question if it's me that has pushed her into these types of moods. It's not often but right now it is my concern and once again I can't release the fact that it's around one of my times of yearning. I find myself pondering about the "how" and "why" of my wife's disintegrating passion to be with me. What we do is nothing different from most people who indulge in intimacy, but it is ours to cherish. We have experimented through trial and error to figure out what we each like best and otherwise. It has been through this trial and error which has drawn us closer. So it's no wonder I have developed the feeling over time that I've probably worn her out. Again, this is not literally, but in the sense of the moment being lost in just being an act of release. There is no passion leading up to fulfillment, just the act of nurturing or completing a task for relief. Such like the one you would have as thirst. I thirst, I seek fulfillment, so I drink. I need to be relieved so I too, need. It makes complete sense to me!

In light of my circumstances, I have continued to find ways to tempt myself through my favorite websites. It is tricky to have out in the open a website page along the taskbar on the computer while another page is open on display. If the person passing by got too close to the computer and could decipher the names across the taskbar, or the acronyms, then my cover would be blown. To remedy that, I often open bogus pages of excel reports, word documents and even pictures so that I would have so many windows of documents open that this would hide the names of websites and couldn't be noticed. Another way that has been successful is I've had more than one tab opened simultaneously on one window. However, I have to be careful when I reopen the page because the wrong website could be opened instead of the bogus one I had on the additional tabs. I've tried on several occasions this act, with some degree of success, only having to end my session in the initial stages. Late nights were the only time that I could make any attempt at allowing my prison to find some release. My only problem with that was I had to keep the door closed to the back room and making certain that the light in the room was filtered by blocking the light under the door. I've attempted this effort a few times only to have the filtered light alert my children of activity that sparked their curiosity and eventually alerting my wife. To no avail I continue to make an attempt at completing this task and staying alert at all times of the opportunity. It has only been four days and slowly going on number five.

This is why when I think back, I can't believe how my aunt would get away with her acts of fulfillment with me and no one ever blinked an eye. She was very good and probably had a good sense of movement calculation or something in order to pull off the close encounters she had with me. She could initiate a moment with my sisters and my cousins in the same room! Everyone around would continue their array of happiness, excitement and would ignore the obvious indicators.

My aunt's ability to be crafty at cloak and dagger was evident on a particular night when my cousin, our sisters and I were playing a game marked out on the wood floor of my grandmother's bedroom with tape. This game was called in the neighborhood at the time, "deadblock". The game consisted of plucking plastic tops of varying sizes filled with tar (asphalt) or wax, across a drawn enclosed board surrounding blocks with numbers on the perimeter and other grouped blocks of numbers within the center. These numbers were enclosed in large squares and strategically placed around the board. This was always done on one of the side streets of the inner city, which were small and usually contained parked cars on one side and was a one way street. On these streets there was rarely any traffic that passed through the street. Many of us just hung around sitting on the curbs viewing the game, waiting for our turn. The difficulty came in having some marking material that could be removed after the game was played a few times. It took raining a few days or consistent traffic to erase the marks. It was very rare that we could play this game inside.

In this particular instant, we had just come inside for the night from playing outside. When we came inside we were trying to figure out a way to continue where we had left off outside in our game of "deadblock". We start to argue about the game because we never finished it. But because my cousin and I would escalate our arguments, my grandmother sent us upstairs to work it out and this allowed us to devise a way to continue the game. By doing this, we indirectly understood that should one of us have a problem that could not be resolved among us, then we could no longer play for the evening. Having that understanding, we played quietly as to not bring any attention to our game. However, we still argued as best as we could quietly.

On this particular night as we played, eventually, our sisters came upstairs to first inquire about the game and then reminded us that they too were playing with us earlier outside. We decided to allow them to join us. As we played, my aunt came into the room and she too inquired about our board game. She asked in different ways about having the desire to join our game, or better yet, posing a competition of the males versus the females or any other combination. My cousin and I explained how we didn't like the odds and if we were to continue that the numbers per side would at least have to be even. Our sisters agreed and gave us our younger sisters. My cousin argued and wanted only our aunt and that that would even the sides. I wanted to oppose but I knew something would happen if I did.

As the feeling from my aunt's presence subsided and the game became so competitively even, I forgot about how often my aunt would hug and kiss on my cousin for any accomplishment or, I, which we made for our team. Eventually we won and some arguing ensued to which my aunt mediated the trouble and sent our sisters away for the moment. She explained that they could come back when they stopped the bickering and when she decided that they had learned their lesson.

My cousin, my aunt and I were left in the room and the mood quickly changed to where my aunt started to play with us in a wrestling manner. Again, my cousin in his naïve understanding went along with this act. I was reluctant the entire time, knowing what was to come of this next; at least this was my belief. As my aunt began allowing my cousin to hold, grab, touch and feel on her in order to gain some leverage, I put an end to the moment. I yelled and started a fight with my cousin for no apparent reason. My cousin interpreted my behavior as a form of jealously for whatever reason. He liked the fact that I showed no hesitation in trying to stop the moment from occurring.

But my aunt was more intrigued of my act of jealously, so she thought of it as such an appealing act. My mannerism moved her so much that she too became upset with my cousin, slapped him on his hands, and as he began to cry, she sent him downstairs and told me to stay for a moment. How she changed the tone of the moment shocked me and I was not prepared for what was to happen next.

She looked about as if she was searching for something in the air, all the while listening for some sort of activity. When she was assured of the activity downstairs, she then explained to me that this moment had to be quick, the "let's play". I pleaded with her that we would get caught; hoping she would concede and we wouldn't have to go through with this session. As usual, she directed me to get under the bed sheets and pull down my pants and underwear, but not to take them off. I wish I had had on shoes on this day. But, she instructed me to hurry up and climb into the bed. She was moving into the bed so fast that I was still trying to pull down my pants. I tried desperately to delay the encounter but after she removed her top, she began to work on me. My aunt pulled one of her legs out of her panties and as she laid in bed on her side, in front me, she started to back up against me.

Under the covers I started to smell the tomato odor again. At the same time this occurred, my cousin and our sisters came back into the room to explain that our grandmother sent them back upstairs to work out our problem. They also informed our grandmother that our aunt allowed me to stay upstairs. This explanation did not deter our grandmother's intent on making certain that we work out our differences. So our grandmother explained that my being allowed to stay upstairs was a privilege for not causing or instigating the trouble.

Now as my cousin, who is now mad at me, and our sisters gathered around the bed, my aunt explained that they could play the game again and that she was playing doctor on me for the moment. I was terrified that we were going to be found out and that I was going to get the beating of my life from our grandmother. My aunt tried to soothe me and this emotion of mine by whispering in my ear that what we were about to do would never be found out. I didn't look in her direction, but instead I stared at some fixture on the wall above the dresser across from the foot of the bed.

So as my cousin and our sisters restarted their game my aunt performed our game on me. This time we played from the side by her placing me on two pillows side by side to elevate me to her side level. She pressed up against me again with her back towards me and lifted up one of legs and placed me in between. As she moved about, my cousin's sister stood up and asked if they could participate in the doctor game. My aunt, without hesitation, allowed all of them to enter the bed from her side, some at her feet and some at her head. She also explained that we all had to be quite and not to move too much. I kept wondering why no one else smelled the odor and made a comment about it. The smell was not pungent, but long enough to make you wonder about the origin. It entered my nostrils periodically. I had hoped that our moment of engagement would be hindered with the acknowledgement of the odor.

To this day I cannot understand how no one present on that day never inquired about the odor or the movement my aunt made. I also wondered with great concern about how she held me in place, played and talked with my cousin and our sisters all at the same time! Even when I tried to cause some one to notice through my mistakes in our involvement, no one paid me any attention. This has always frustrated me.

I've tried to put together many of the moments that I had to endure and looked at extensively how no one saw, heard or sensed that I had a problem or that my aunt was the problem. Even in my encounters with my cousin, our arguing, our petty fights, everyone dismissed them as related to sibling rivalry. I had to protect my cousin. I often wondered about my efforts to protect my cousin for as long as I could. I tried so hard to prevent him from experiencing a similar fate. However, that day I remember vividly because that was the first day I would've physically beaten my cousin, caused him real bodily harm in order to save him from being infected. Unfortunately, it would not be the last.

In addition, what made this encounter more acute to me was how enlightened I'd become to my surroundings. At least this was my understanding as I grew and reflected on the many encounters. As I have aged, this intuition has brought me to an awareness that I made me wonder did I really have a gift at such a young age? When I recall my moments as I've done over time before trying to suppress them, I have seen this understanding demonstrated right before my eyes. I was amazed at my effort to stay focused on the encounter at hand with my aunt and to give no indication of my true intentions. Even when I would once again be subjected by her with my new prison, I was able to foresee the moment up to the end before it was initiated. I felt this understanding alone belong to me at least this was my perception I believed to be a part of me back then. This sense instilled in me a feeling of pride of some sort, because I had in my possession something no one else had but my aunt.

At my age then, I thought, I would find refuge, solace from my prison. It amazed me to the point that I believed I could not share such a gift because no one would understand, no one would believe it was really happening. But those thoughts would always take me back to my having this so called understanding that I received from indulging with my provider. I had truly lost my innocence and by losing it, I was provided with some sense that I was reluctant to indulge.

My intuition was my essence, my sense of place, time and this perception became my protector, for I learned how to avoid encounters long enough to cause some anger within my aunt. In other future encounters, that ability would cause me more pain. To say the least, it was because I had not yet perfected the true understanding of the entire ordeal was where I lost the battle of whit and thus cause myself pain. My mind had not broadened beyond what I had experienced, seen, heard. But my aunt, well, she was more astute in her learning about what I was possibly thinking, or perceived. Often times, she was able to counter my moves, my conversations of anxiety with other family members who were in our midst before she made me endure the game, our game, the…"let's play". It would take more time to counter her counter and until that time would occur, she held the authority, the additional understanding and the opinion from the other adults that at my age then, children often made stories of grandeur or harshness in order to be noticed, seen and involved. In other ways some family members were of the understanding that children are seen and not heard.

It was a hard time for me to fathom this perception, but I fought hard and often to change the adage. Unfortunately, I was never able to be a victor in that approach and this caused me some bitterness to continue in length, sustainable relationships with family. In other words, I will always interact with family, but I tolerate them only for a time. Our subjects of conversation only stayed across the surface and when things turned more personal, I could sensed there was either more to talk about or nothing at all. I just never wanted to venture down the road for fear of exposing my prison. I would be embarrassed and ashamed of my actions. As I write this, I can feel the chills of being found. I just realized that as I write this…my hands are shaking…

Immoderation

I had anticipated that there would be more people walking around back and forth looking for the desire of their monetary dreams. The noise wasn't as loud as I've experienced in the past and there was not as much smoke. Between the three of us I believe we had already downed three good drinks. I was feeling the second and the third and wanted to relax a moment. So my cousin, his friend and my neighbor stopped their standing and looking around to sit down next to me. I had taken my single seat off the bar and away from the tables in order to have a better view and to not be disturbed by some other patron looking for visual love, I mean lust. But my cousin, his buddy and my neighbor found me.

As we sat trying to figure out who had change for a twenty dollar bill, my cousin alerted me to the next act that was coming up to the stage. Before the voluptuous lady could start into her act, my cousin's friend nudged me from my left side to imply that I should calm down my neighbor. My neighbor had started to show some signs of being mesmerized and we didn't want him to go home without at least some of his money he was about to lose. My neighbor had a habit of spending in excess at times (don't ask how I know). His eyes followed the woman's every move as she danced and walked about the stage.

Again, during this fiasco I kept wondering why my neighbor wanted me to join him to go out on the town. This is the same person I try not to have a lengthy conversation whenever I leave my house. I had avoided him with different excuses that sounded legitimate up to this point. To my understanding, I think he needed a sure alibi and a cohort who wouldn't blow his cover. However, this night, he approached me as I was entering my home with my cousin and my cousin's friend for a simple night of sports watching. My cousin in his lustful manner could not pass up the chance once my neighbor started implying about a trip to a gentleman's club. My cousin's friend had suggested many locations which amazed me of his knowledge of the names and the locations of these places. We had finally settled on one that my neighbor had never visited, but always wanted to explore. He was so excited and thankful that I had taken him up on his offer that he offered to pay my entrance and some incidentals that I would incur when we arrived. It amazed me that he had such knowledge of this particular place as if he had been there before on some other night.

She approached me from a side that was out of my peripheral vision and caught me by surprise. Her movements were a complete surprise to me and my reaction was sudden. She was not amused by my jittery movement and calmly preceded with her agenda. I showed my displeasure toward her because I didn't want to pay her for services that I didn't request. She even ignored that demonstration by me and was of the understanding that no one in this establishment would refuse her. I tried not to allow her to come closer to me and she never stopped in her approach. Unfortunately, she just wasn't my type, she looked good, but she just wasn't my type. However, she explained she had just started the night and wanted to give me the only "freebie" of the night. She said I looked "cute", whatever. As she began dancing in front of me, I could not be moved but I admitted to myself and the fellas later, that she was good at her job, at least up to that point. Her dance led her to straddle my lap and she did. In her sitting on me she looked at me with a sultry expression and pressed herself up against me with subtle jesters. This fair lady tried and tried again to place my hands and fingers in places I did not feel comfortable with her. I tried to oblige her respectfully, but she kept up her pursuit. This act was enticing, but, I was not amused because of my prison. Should my prison awake, I would have to engage this fair lady into an act where I would have to pay dearly for her services. Then again, I wasn't sure if she would like to embark on such a business transaction. Finally, I don't think I could go through because despite my lust, I do love and care for my wife, though moments like these are conflicting. So I tried not to alert the fair lady of reluctance. In the meantime, I could hear in the immediate distant the guys (my cousin, his friend and my neighbor) laughing and "ooh-ing" at my uncomfortable circumstances. They started to cheer and edge me on to do other things with the lady. Eventually, she leaned over, still straddling me, whispered in my ear to calm me down and relax, because she wasn't going to hurt me. She was in full bloom with her act and waited for any response from me. I laughed at her pun and simply tried to reason with her when she again leaned over and questioned me why I didn't want to play.

As I would later move about the various scenes of enticement and over indulging, I found a secluded seat near the bar to just relax. Really I couldn't relax, but I tried. While sitting in area where there was a view to a circle stage, a few guys had come in to the place to celebrate a groom to be, by summoning a few ladies. The guys walked past me and gathered just off to my right at a table just in front of the bar. As the groom to be, sat in anticipation, the women gathered around him and his friends began to cheer. In the midst of this action, I caught the eye of one of the ladies. She winked at me and I smiled and she continued on employing her part of the action. I couldn't stop my visual fixation on her because she looks like someone I know. The longer I sat there watching all the movement around, over and under the groom to be, and friends, I stayed focused on this girl. Eventually she ignored me but I wouldn't let up my stare. When she smiled at one of the friends of the groom to be, it hit me…she resembled what my niece could look like at her age. This was something I wasn't prepared to view, or was it again, my imagination of hopeful things? I moved to a spot where the rest of this group couldn't see me and waited. Finally, I lost sight of the girl, but I tried to look for her from my seat, standing and looking over the crowd, then peering between the movements of the people.

I had caused the fellas to become uncomfortable after that incident with the first lady because the bouncers kept passing by them and standing in the proximity of their enjoyment. I had ruined the night to some degree. They each questioned me at different times throughout the rest of the night about what I had said to the young lady dancing over me. I never mentioned what I had said exactly, but rather I explained that the lady became upset with my persistence in explaining that I wasn't going to pay for her services. They would laugh about this and call me cheap. But the lady had struck a nerve and I reacted too soon in calling her a foul name. In all the places to call someone a foul name because you're upset with their services! I could've gone somewhere else in the building with another lady or just sat there in disgust. But the encouragement of the last lady that resembled my niece kept me wondering and enticed until we had reached our moment of departure. We then left the warehouse place of so called indulging pleasures without confrontation, we smelled like used up cigarettes or cigars and bad alcohol breathe.

My cousin parked his car between my neighbor's house and my house along the curb. My neighbor and I both got out simultaneously from both sides in the rear and I stopped to close out the night with a quick conversation with my cousin. Meanwhile my neighbor hesitated, then waved goodbye, then slowly made his way up his driveway to his door. I could feel he wanted to be included in the last conversation. My cousin gestured for me to come over to the driver's side to inquire about my unhappy attitude. I informed him that young lady wanted me to pay in spite of her initially giving me the free service. He laughed, his friend laughed and I snickered to appease them. I added that there were other better looking women in that place and some of them wanted to take the experience to the next step. My cousin explained to his friend that I was all hype and no bite. We all laughed at his affirmation and I started to leave. Meantime, I could see my neighbor lagging at his entryway hoping to hear something which would include his participation.

Inside I was once again holding back my prison as if I had held my bladder too long. I tried to calm myself as to not cause twitching and jerking within my body. Once I calmed down, I was now to a point where I could move about in a casual manner. However, my prison moved like a measured frenzy through my body similar to a slow boil. It was a tickling heat that caused me to feel a moisten feeling about various areas on my skin. I began my preparation to unleash my prison. But my wife announced her presence somewhere along the second floor near the stairs. She inquired about my evening out and I responded with little details. My wife suspected I was tired and probably a little drunk. To ease her concern, I began this long and elaborate story of not being able to concentrate on having fun with the guys because I had work on my mind the entire time. My wife's next line of questioning was to find out if I needed something to relax, like her company or allowing me to verbally vent my anguish. I instantly became upset, trying not to alarm her because she didn't offer nor implied for us to indulge ourselves in a moment of passion. As she now descended the stairs, I could see the outlining of her teddy pajamas and assumed right away that this was why she was approaching me. Unfortunately, more disappointing feelings developed within me, and she tried in a lethargic manner to assure me that whatever concerned me would be alright by tomorrow. She reached up and slowly moved her arms under my arms and pulled me close to her. She looked up and tried to give me a small peck on the lips when she smelled the alcohol and the smell of cigarettes. She knew there were only two places that I would have visited that gave that smell. She knew me too well. We verbally danced around my latest venture and I tried to explain my participation but she wasn't moved by my efforts. My wife, she didn't want to argue nor indulge in being upset because it was late and she wanted me to tell her what was my next move. I couldn't enter the bedroom with an odor like this on my body and clothes. I would have to change downstairs then shower once I was upstairs before getting into bed.

Upstairs, I countered with my wife the need to go back to work to finish this job that was on my mind. She refused my suggestion and with a sultry voice, persuaded me to stay and come to bed. I followed her suggestion and when I was finally prepared to move under the covers, she was asleep. In all the time we have been married and courting, I never took advantage of my wife while she slept. I thought about it many nights and tried to persuade her out of her sleep, but tonight I just didn't have the strength to awaken her.

As I laid hugging her close to me and feeling her becoming more comfortable in my arms, I tried to use this moment to "lull" myself to sleep. I had trouble from the start and with my wife pressed up against me wasn't helping at all. I could feel her warmth and soft features and it awakened my prison. I had hoped I could awaken her with my new growth, but she wasn't moved and the unsettling feeling rose again within me. I pressed up against her gyrating a bit to encourage her, but it seemed to calm her all the more.

I started to push away slowly and my wife refused to move as she slept. As I waited for her to settle in again, I moved methodically from under her, then out of the bed, placing the covers in a position as to not alarm her of the new, cool air under the sheets and found some athletic clothes. All I had to do now was to ease out of the bedroom, down the hall pass the other bedrooms and prepare for my prison. I did this by slipping on some shorts that were laid at the foot of the bed and stepped into my slippers. I then eased the door to the closed position by holding the knob in the open position until the door lightly tapped the door jamb. From there I methodically ease into each step I took, pausing in between each. As I entered the back room, I thought I heard movement in the hallway. I waited, frozen in place, breathing with my mouth open wide and easing my breath from my lungs. I started to look about to enhance my concentration. Nothing. I then eased the door to the backroom closed by again holding the knob in the open position until the door lightly tapped the door jamb. Then I slowly turned the lock in the knob to close. I switched the knob into the locked position. Next, I turned on the computer and shifted the monitor over to one side so that I could get a glimpse of any activity at the door. I waited for the system programs to boot, when there was a light rap at the door. In the midst of my excitement, I almost panicked. But I waited to imply that I assumed I heard a sound but wasn't sure. Again I could hear a light rap at the door.

In disgust I arose and slowly made my way to the door and tried not to unlock the handle without a sound, then I turned the knob and opened…I could barely see her in the dark. She reached out to me and finally caught my hand. I tugged in the opposite direction to indicate that she should enter this room with me. She walked in, moved pass me to the computer and she knelled down to turn it off before it could boot. She reached up to me and I moved to lean down to her. That's when she began to kiss me on my neck with an open mouth. In the process, I could feel her sultry breathe as a slow rising warmth. It felt good, smooth, enticing. Her breath always had a peculiar smell of a feminine quality but I could never relate it to anything. It was the kind of odor that only a woman possesses and it always held my attention when we were just small increments away from one another. I turned to kiss her…my wife began to squirm in an uneasy fashion…I had indeed fallen asleep.

The next day my wife had rewarded me with a loving wife's passion that I was missing. All the while we tried to stay quiet because we kept hearing activity throughout the house outside the door. The voices moved back and forth, nearing the door but never coming to the door. **They** were up and pretty soon someone was going to knock on our door. We continued like young people trying not to get caught at something. We laughed about our undertaking, hushing one another, snickering at times and just smiling at the notion. How does she know me so well? She has foiled my prison, again. Thank you.

However, later in the day, my prison has alerted me again. Apparently it was not totally fulfilled and needed more to be completely satisfied. But my opportunity to bring about the desired act to fruition wasn't available. My weekend was now surrounded by movement, besides; I was tired from lack of sleep the night before and tired from my wife this morning.

Eventually I made my way downstairs to eat, when I was summoned to the living room by my wife. I explained that I wanted to finish my breakfast made with such caring hands and then I'd join them. When I did finish and entered the living room there on the couch sat my wife and my eldest daughter. There was setup in this arrangement but I didn't know what the plan was. My wife insisted that I join them to get my opinion on a show regarding family matters. I assured them this was not my expertise and wanted to at the very least, prepare some sort of lunch for myself for later. They continued with my joining them. Eventually I did and my wife wanted me to "cuddle" but I wanted to prepare my afternoon meal. So, on the floor, I watched the television. It was a story where a couple could not be seen in public because of their reputations and how one friend sought to destroy their relationship by subjecting both of them with unwanted passion. I moved quickly to rise and forage through the kitchen until I found something which would satisfy me until my lunch time. However, this bite led me to stay put on the floor longer, where, again, sleep became one of my good friends.

…my aunt was spending the weekend with one of her girlfriends and wasn't to return for a few days. I thought my cousin and I would find some relief that day but as we played with some friends this day would change.

Many of the children in the neighborhood were out that day and we played many games; jacks, jump rope, step ball, wall ball, a card game called "war" and others. It was just excitement everywhere you turned until some of the boys started teasing the girls jumping rope. They had instigated the girls to chase them about the area. It was innocent until one of the boys grabbed one of the girls in an inappropriate manner. At first nothing was said about it until it started happening again and again. Eventually some one thought it would be best if we played another game, this game called "catch a girl-get a girl". Innocent as it may sound, it was the kind of game that promoted actions that could be looked at as assault. It was a game of child-like lustfulness. This game conjured up actions that would embarrass parents to know that their little darlings had some idea how to instigate the workings of intercourse. Most of the time when the girl was caught, you got to kiss her or hug her ever so tight. On other occasions the boy or boys got the opportunity to rub or feel on the girl. Yes, these are the practices of the possibilities. Many of the girls didn't want to play and some of the boys likewise.

My cousin was somewhere in the middle of the commotion when he called to me to join him. Not to refuse my partner in crime, my cousin, I joined in, only to be lost in the scramble. When I finally got my bearings I noticed a new comer or visitor to our neighborhood. She was beautiful, caramel skin with short hair. I stood within the crowd just staring at her mesmerized. Something within me urged me to be with her for no other reason than to be with her. I formulated my plan to be with her and waited for the girls to run in all directions. I spotted her running away from the group of girls she started with and put my plan into action. So without delay, I chased her and chased her and chased her some more. She was fast and alluding. Her long legs seemed to not stop as she casually darted about the streets. When I finally caught her by the arm, other boys tried to take her away from me. She refused their advances and tried to show reluctance as I pulled lightly on her. Some of the other boys tried to pull me away from to discourage her, but she held firm in her decision. As I approached her again, several boys tried with one last gasp to come between us, but it didn't work. They started to walk away from us when one of the boys in the crowd noticed more girls running and off they went in that direction. As I held her hand, she never moved away and just waited for the next step from me. I was looking for a secluded place to take her in hand with me. As I scanned the neighborhood, and eventually found our spot, I tugged on her and she followed without hesitation. The walk was short but we had to maneuver around some of the other groups of boys and girls. Most of them didn't even notice us. The ones that did notice us ignore our movements.

She was more nervous than I but she looked at me trustingly. I asked her was her name and she asked me the same question right after I'd asked her. We exchanged names and I could tell she wasn't interested in what I had to say. So, I proposed a kiss to her and she asked me if I had bad breath. I've always laughed about this part of my memory. I explained no, but asked the same question and she used this act to become offended. At this point I began to show concern and curiosity as to why I couldn't reciprocate the same question. She ignored me and turned her head away from me. That's when I reached out to her, held her hand, pulled her close to me, looked her dead in her eyes and kissed her. My kiss started out as just pressing my lips up to hers. She didn't refused and rather seemed enthusiastic about the engagement. I tried to insert my tongue slowly and again she didn't refuse my advances. This is the other part I remember so vividly, we started to close our eye, and turned our heads from side to side slowly. I tried not to allow any saliva to peek out of the corners of mouth. We continued this act for it seems an eternity.

However, I had gone too far in practicing what had evolved into my prison. The urge to move my prison into the next phase was slowly taking over me and I enjoyed the rush of emotion it released in me. At first, I placed my hands in places the girl felt a little uncomfortable but she allowed me as long as I moved slow and stayed on the outside of her underclothes. She told me this by holding my hand several times as I moved in those directions. She felt soft in all the places I placed my hands even though I also felt material. Next, my uncertainty in moving forward alarmed her because I became a little forceful in my actions. I had succumbed to my prison full fledge and was almost of my own mind. I had unbuttoned her summer slacks and moved them halfway past her buttocks. She wiggled a little to assist me. I was reaching for her panties when she began to softly ask me to stop there and to go no further. I kept kissing on her all the while, on her cheeks, and her neck. Whatever had become of my mannerism and respect went out the door with the surge of my feelings. I had one had below her waist and my other hand was now up under her shirt and what I thought was her bra. I startled myself because I didn't know I could remember so much of what I had been taught. In all of this movement and kissing I was able to get the girl's panties to about her mid thigh. Because I recognized her acceptance, I proceeded with trying to move my pants past my buttocks.

I should've stopped, but it was like an incessant rage that had no end but only an agenda. Before I could go further, I don't know what I would have done next; we heard other kids in the distant and quickly dressed. I looked back in their immediate direction to determine if we needed anymore time, but they were still in pursuit. When dressed ourselves in time and we could still hear the voices in the distance. At first I didn't want to look at her to find out how she felt about the moment. She tried not to look in my direction. After we made sure we looked presentable, I looked at her and asked her was she feeling any different. She said yes, and I asked her how she was feeling different. The girl explained that she at first she liked what we were doing but then she became a little afraid of me and that she knew what we were doing was wrong, but she didn't know how to stop me. Then, after she explained that, she started to cry and I tried to console her. I reached out to her and gave her a big hug. I held her close to me, looking out into space wondering about the moment. I apologized for my actions and she forgave me.

This girl continued to play games with me, I believe we even talked on occasion; she would hug me in fun, laugh and cry with me. I don't remember crying much, but I do remember her crying. We vowed to never speak of the moment nor tell of the moment. She was always a bit shy and cautious around me after that incident. I never forgot that she forgave me for trying to infect her and from that point on we stayed friends but at some distant. It was the summer I turned ten years of age.

Derivation

Today at work the day seemed to go by slowly as if to taunt me into thinking that I'm missing something important. I have two assignments that are current on my desk and they require more attention from me, but I lack the motivation necessary to start. I can't figure out why I'm so lethargic today. In the moment, I try to think of the many encounters that have occupied my day thus far as if these moments will yield unfound answers. At this very moment, nothing seems to stand out.

I've paced my cubicle like some caged animal being mindful not to draw attention when I extend my arms too far above my space. I am in deep thought trying to find the spark of encouragement I need to finish the day and to then evaluate the "why" this moment has occurred. As I move about, trying to replay events regarding the cost summary and the current timelines of this project I can't help but notice that I've never had any visual stimulation in my space. As I contemplate why this is a new found fact, I deviate to the possibility of having the wrong type of pictures as my reason for not having any pictures. My mind ventures to the edge of perversion but I catch myself before I entertain that thought. But as I acknowledge this found fact, I realize that I don't even have pictures of my family. This revelation causes me to sit and to contemplate why I haven't decorated my cubicle with family pictures or any other. My eventual conclusion is that I don't want to personalize something that is temporary in my possession with something that has permanency. On the other hand I rationalize that I'm trying to shelter my family from curious and inquisitive people. This thought made some sense but then I further conclude that I could be embarrassed in some way of their (my family) existence. I try to convince myself that installing the pictures would be a respectable gesture and that I should get started on trying to find pictures that would stimulate conversation regarding my family. A task not out of reach and would help me along the way in dealing with moments of being in a funk, like this one in particular.

So I try again to sort through the cost summary of this one project, cross referencing it with the current timelines and as I find the spark that I can use to push myself along, I decide to start my playlist of songs and put on my headphones to add to my new found motivation. From my chair I swivel back and forth, tapping here and there as I work through the assignment. I've allowed myself to slip further into my setting by mumbling the words to songs when a colleague taps on a partition of my cubicle and stands at the entryway for acknowledgement. To my unfortunate contentment, I haven't notice him…yet. I would later find out how much he enjoyed my gyrations, gestures and the many facial expressions tied into the moment of the song. Oh he was thoroughly entertained and began his blackmailing suggestions in jest.

He wanted me to first brief him on the summaries and the corresponding timelines as well as giving me the first notice of the new female working in the documentation section. All in a brief statement, I almost missed the last part. He laughed at my inability to focus on more than one thing at a time. So after I briefed him as to what would be in our report, he pulled from behind one of his arms he kept behind his back, his portion of the report and again asked me about the girl in the same statement. Frustrated with his subliminal messages, I gave up and asked him why I should be concerned with this new employee. He stated that she would be working closely with our department in order to expedite some of the delays that were developing as part of the filing projects. This fact was of interest to me, but I was more concerned if this new employee was to be fulltime or part-time. He went on to explain that she would be full time but that she would start her first assignment with us then she would be evaluated as to where she would continue employment. Now that she was on my mind I asked more questions, but instead of directly answering them, my coworker included physical descriptions of the new worker. This exchange went on for a moment until my office phone rang.

When I answered and found that it was my wife, I waved off my coworker who tried to distract me with hand descriptions of the new female worker. My wife has impeccable timing. I tried not to study my coworker's descriptions and focus on my wife.

She started to ask me a question but then continued in a story fashion of how another family outing would be great if we went to the movies. It sounded like a good idea but I wondered what we all could watch as a movie. She had several suggestions and said she was already discussing this with the kids and they were starting to agree on a few choices. They had gone along since they hadn't been out since the last time and thought it was about time. My niece was excited about the thought. However, I wasn't convinced but I went along because it was true we hadn't been out since the last time and since my wife had gone through the trouble to make it possible.

I ended our phone conversation and again became engulfed with my latest project at work. To my surprise I would complete it before the end of the work day. My coworker would later say he came past again to agitate me but he saw how efficiently I was working and thought otherwise. Besides he would later tell me that he thought my wife called probably with some surprising news for me later after work. He guessed well but missed the mark.

On my train ride home I contacted my wife to give her my whereabouts. She regretted to tell me that the show would start close to the time I would be arriving home and that I wouldn't have time to change. I became a bit irritated at the fact that I would now have to attend a movie showing in a suit and I felt uncomfortable, overdressed. She reminded me of my commitment to have family time and that she would have to owe me. All I could do was laugh at the bargain. So as I disembark the train, I tried to plan out if I indeed had enough time to change, but thought otherwise since my wife had made the arrangements. As I walked toward the car I began thinking about her impeccable timing to prevent me from indulging in the conversation about the new female worker. I tried to dismiss it as I got into my car and tried to take the shortest route to home.

Upon arrival home, it looked as if some kind of accident had occurred. My wife yelled to me from the kitchen and I could hear the girls upstairs yelling at one another that there wasn't any more time since I was home. My wife kept yelling in my direction that she too would have to wear her clothes from work and that she had arrived home about forty five minutes ago and wanted to prepare her lunch for work tomorrow. She yelled again and asked me if I wanted her to make me something for work tomorrow. I conceded with a yes and tried to ignore the gesture. I waited at the foyer and heard no sign of my son. So as I tried to sit I could hear him coming upstairs from the basement snickering at how the girls were acting. We sat for a few minutes and talked about how he enjoyed his work day and he asked me the same. We laughed as if we were two businessmen chatting up another day. So we waited a little more for them.

We all piled into my car and off went to the theatre. To my surprise the lines were short and the crowds were few. We ordered some popcorn and drinks because I was told that we were going out afterwards to eat. That was okay by me. As we entered the seating, the kids darted off in one direction and we found a two seater so as to prevent anyone stepping past us for their seats. Then the credits began to roll and my wife snuggled up next to me. I pushed back the arm rest between us and she threw her legs over mine. I whispered to her that we could try anything here because of the different lighting. She looked at me with a little disappointment. We continued to snuggle and enjoy the movie.

The movie turned out to be a mystery that had us all talking about what we thought would've happened or who wasn't our initial suspect. It was enjoyable and I made the kids thank my wife for her choice. I mentioned to all of them that I didn't think the kids would've have gone to watch this movie on their own, it just didn't seem their type. After saying that I got sneers and complaints about my comment and we walked toward the car. My wife had me drive a few blocks away to a restaurant that had valet parking. I became concerned because I thought because of the valet that the prices on the menu would reflect as costly. She explained that this was a gratuity of the restaurant in order to make the guests feel welcome and more relaxed which meant that the patrons might stay a little longer and spend more. I started to ask where she found this place but left it alone.

We were greeted and escorted to our table along the raised floor in toward the right of the entry. We got a table near by the window and could see traffic and people moving about, interesting. Our waitress came over and took our drink orders and made some suggestions regarding the appetizers as well as what were the specials for this evening. The kids couldn't agree on more than three types of appetizers, so my wife ordered two. I explained that we should order our meals now because it appeared that the restaurant was filling with other patrons. The kids looked about and agreed and tried to decide as quickly as they could on their meals. My wife and I order similar meals and the waitress reiterated it back to be certain, made corrections and left. As soon as she left the kids spoke about the ambiance of the restaurant and how it made them feel "classy". They continued inquiring how a place like this would cost. My wife and I laughed at them and she explained that it's not every day we can go out like this but when we do we like to go to local restaurants. By saying that my wife had impressed them well and we continued with the hypothesizing about the movie.

However after we started to eat the appetizers I noticed my girls whispering and then my youngest gestured to my wife and she leaned over to inquire. I tried to continue small talk about the movie and my niece explained that she would have never thought my wife and I would pick that type of movie. My son interjected that at times we can be as mainstream as if were still trying to stay connected with the young crowd. We laughed and my wife explained to me that she had to use the restroom and that the girls would have to go with her. I didn't look concerned but as I moved out of my seat for her all the girls followed and once again it was just me and my son. For a moment it was awkward, two males at a large table. I mentioned to my son that I would have to plan a night where he and I would hang out. He decided to pick fun at this suggestion and asked me if I would plan something like this, a movie and dinner. I said no, it would be more like a sporting event and then go get something to eat. He asked how different a movie was from a sporting event. He had me there, but I explained he's my son and we haven't been out in a while. I waited for him to dissect my offer and then he asked if we went somewhere could he have a beer. I thought at least he asked, so I said we would look into this but if he told his mother the deal was off. Just then my wife came back with the girls and she explained to me that our oldest wasn't feeling well, that it wasn't that time of the month and she suspects that it might have been the popcorn. I said to her that no one seems to be sick and that we all ate from the same tub. She said no that the kids ate from a different one and that was her concern. I looked up and tried to gage the kids' reactions. No one seemed affected but my youngest.

The rest of the evening at dinner was awkward because my oldest tried to eat and everyone seemed concerned about her wellbeing. After our meals were served I decided it was best for us to receive carryout on all the food because we had to leave. The waitress motioned for me to excuse myself from the table to ask a question. She wanted to know if any of the appetizers or drinks had made anyone sick, I explained no and that this occurred before we arrived. She was relieved and since we weren't going to stay any longer she wanted the manager to speak with us to maybe offer some sort of gratuity for a later visit. I thanked her gave her an additional cash tip in hand along with the one I was going to leave when I paid for the meals. She didn't know about that one.

My son and I carried the bags outside and waited for the valet to return with the car. That's when I noticed my oldest moving toward the bushes and my wife holding her. She was vomiting in the bushes. My youngest and my niece were starting to panic. I assured them that all was well and told my son to keep an eye out for the car. When my oldest finally finished, I sent my youngest and my niece inside to get some wet and dry paper towels. It seemed forever as we waited for the girls to return but as they returned, the valet was pulling up toward us with the car. I instructed my son to pay the valet with the tip I gave him, get in and pop the trunk. Meanwhile my wife and the girls kept their attention on my oldest. By the time my son and I loaded the take out neatly in the trunk, my wife explained to me that our oldest would be alright and that she would just need some rest. My wife got into the back seat with our oldest, my son sat up front and we drove off for home.

It was good for us that the restaurant was not far from where we lived. When we entered the driveway, my oldest was at it again, vomiting in the grass along our driveway. The other kids were making queasy sounds as a reaction, and I sent them in the house. My wife explained she would go in the house to retrieve some other clothes for my oldest and a bucket for just in case. I waited next to my oldest until she finished. She looked up at me with such embarrassment that I was embarrassed. I started to tell her that there was no one around and that it was okay, because I did it once. I thought I was lying to her, but I thought about a time in school in which I did the very exact same thing. It took me a moment to recall a moment, but I did. My wife came out and escorted my oldest into the garage, closed it behind them and motioned for me to enter the house from the front door.

In side I met my wife and oldest in the hallway off the kitchen that links the garage. My oldest now appeared to have that nauseated look of being physically worn out. My wife guided her upstairs and asked me to bring up the bucket she handed me. Upstairs, the kids were mumbling about what happened in my son's room and didn't pay much attention to us as we guided our oldest into her room. My wife stayed with our oldest and I left the two of them alone. As I was closing the door, my youngest appeared and asked me where she would be sleeping tonight because she didn't want to be responsible for my oldest vomiting. I wanted to snicker but explained that she could stay in the bedroom with her cousin. My youngest said she felt "weireded out" if she slept in a bed with another female. I was taken by this statement and paused for a moment to take this statement in as well as to come up with an answer. It hit me and I suggested that the two of them could sleep at opposite ends of the bed. My niece joined and explained that she doesn't like the covers to come off her feet. I turned to answer her statement and my youngest tried to over talk her. A small argument was brewing and I was losing control quickly, because I was surprise at how swift this had occurred. From the room she was occupying, my wife yelled to our youngest that she two choices; her room with her sister and the possibility of her vomiting or with our niece with the covers possibly being moved from over her feet. Peace came swift and so it was settled that my youngest endured my niece, for one night.

Inside our room as my sat upright watching a rerun of one of her detective shows, I tried to get comfortable. I couldn't and sat up to engage my wife in conversation. She obliged and we talked more about the movie, our oldest getting sick and why the other children hadn't had similar symptoms. We explored many ideas about the situations and what might have happened. For now though, she would be fine through the night. I thought about, out loud, about the care we took with her being our first and all the moments of panic we experienced in her early years. We laughed and recalled particular moments. So just before my wife would give into her sleep, she wanted to check on our oldest one more time. I suggested that she should allowed me to do the honors. She smiled and said she would wait for me. I walked down the hall and slowly opened the door of our daughter's room. From afar I could see my oldest snuggled under blankets, breathing heavily. I quietly made my way over to her bedside to check the bucket and how she slept. She moved a little and I backed away, stepped quietly as I tried to navigate my way out of her room. As I entered my bedroom, my wife was on her way to sleep but tried to talk with me. I ignored her and she fell into her sleep. I hurriedly tried to join her.

My aunt had company over to my grands for the first time in…I can't remember. However one of her girlfriends was good looking, at least to my cousin and me. She wore those short jean shorts that are close to male boxers, she wore a tight shirt which revealed the type of bra she wore underneath. In fact the shirt covering her bra was white and her bra was green. This girlfriend had on sandals and had a short haircut. My cousin mentioned to me in a whisper that he doesn't like short hair, but the hairstyle of this girlfriend looked good on her.

We were jealous of the way my aunt and girlfriends played with our sisters and ignored us. On different occasions, we tried to involve ourselves but were either told to leave or ignored to the point we left out of frustration. In a twist of fate, I began hating my aunt girlfriends and tried to persuade my cousin into thinking the same. He too ignored me because he was so infatuated with the girlfriend with the green bra. So my aunt grew tired of us and called our grand to get us to leave until the girlfriends left. My cousin and I played outside on the porch and talked about the girlfriends.

Time past and my grand called us in for the night. While we sat in the living room watching television, my aunt and her girlfriends descended the upstairs to leave. My grands said their goodbyes and so did my aunt's girlfriends. After my aunt re-entered the vestibule, she went into the kitchen to grab a few snacks. We asked about the snacks as she was walking past us to go back upstairs and once again she ignored us.

Eventually from the upstairs, we could hear the same laughter we heard earlier and thought about our aunt engaging our sisters in funny conversations. It didn't make sense, but we went along with the idea. It took some time at least that was how we saw it when our grand was slightly grabbing us by my arms to alert us that it was time to go to bed. So off we went, I was trying not to rub my eyes anymore because they were dry.

The next day we were racing to get up to be the first downstairs for the television, when my cousin alerted me that we had company sleeping in the back room and it was the girlfriend with the green bra. I was shocked and didn't know whether to ask him how he found out or if we should go and take a peek at her. As we go, we decided on the latter.

We made our way down to the hallway checking back periodically for anyone who might be getting up. From there I turned the handle slowly, not letting it go until I could get the door open to a crack. We waited for a response, nothing. So we opened the door slowly but enough so that we could squeeze through. We hit the floor like we were in war and under attack. Again we listened out for sounds, nothing but breathing. My cousin looked over at me and I looked back. He moved over to the other side of the bed at the foot and I, the other side. We looked at one another as we slowly made our way up to the head of the bed by crawling on all fours. Again we waited for sounds, nothing. We were close and we knew if we got this close then we could go all the way. I got up on my knees and waited for my cousin, but since he was shorter than me, he had to fully stand. We gazed at the girlfriend with the green bra sleeping, but she didn't have on the green bra, but a laced teddy. Back then we didn't know it was a teddy but it was sheer enough to see her chest.

The girlfriend's arm was holding the covers in her armpit and the other arm was under her pillow. The covers were just below her chest. My cousin wanted to touch her chest, I gave him the green light and wanted to see between her legs. So while my cousin was softly touching her chest, I eased the covers down past her legs. She moved! We dropped as quietly to the floor as quick as we could! We waited, looking at one another from under the bed. It seemed forever, our wait, so we moved back into position. When we looked at the girlfriend again, she still had one arm under the pillow, but the other arm was across her stomach and her legs were slightly spread. Oh I knew this was my moment. My cousin started back on her chest and by that time, I had one hand over her panties. We were both massaging both areas when I decided to take our venture further and tried to penetrate her with one of my hands. I had finally started penetration....AHAH!

It was too late to drop to the floor, nor did we have time to think of what to do next. Instead my cousin moved to the window and pretended to look outside while I was studying items on the dresser. We were so busted and her voice got louder. We started to lie as to why we were in that room and she screamed for our aunt, I ran out the room, but my cousin wasn't fast enough. As I'm looking back on the scene, he wouldn't have made it anyway, he was on the side of the bed closest to the window and he waould have to pass the bed before getting to the door. The girlfriend held him in her arms and I could hear my cousin scream like a girl. I could hear some tussling and from downstairs, I could see my grands making their way to the backroom. I would eventually see my aunt trying to get her robe on as she too was headed to the backroom. The n came my sisters and cousins. As the commotion reached a pitch, my grand yelled, "Stop this right now now!" There was dead silence and I could hear him telling my aunt to send my sisters and the other girls back to their rooms. Then I could hear my grands speaking with the girlfriend and cousin jumping in with denials. He was told to not utter another word and so the girlfriend started her story.

I would've gotten away with my side of the incident but I could hear my name being called and my aunt walking back toward the room my cousin and I was occupying. She didn't find me and headed toward the steps when she heard the TV. I know her actions to be true cause she paused and snickered then moved down the steps where she stopped to look in my direction. I tried to look surprised but she informed that I should get upstairs…now.

When I arrived to the back room, my cousin had panic written all over his face and I was trying to think of a way out of the matter. As the questions came, I too, began to panic and couldn't keep my story straight. The girlfriend made other accusations which we could not deny because, one, she was older, two, we shouldn't have done what we did, three, we started out lying about what had happen. Eventually we both were chastised with some intense moments and sent to our room. There in our room, we decided she would be forever hated as we tried to lay comfortably on our sore arms and legs. That was the last time my cousin and I ever did anything like that together and as I recount the incident, how did we get into the room without startling the girlfriend or better yet, why didn't she wake while we were touching her and why did she wait until after I had make hands…I think she might have liked some of what we were doing. But alas, we never saw her again.

Indiscretion

"...let's play?"

My daughters wanted to introduce my niece to some of their girlfriends in the neighborhood by having what they called a modern day sleep over. They had convinced my wife of this idea and she seemed to change right before my eyes as if she was one of the girls. It was amazing to see the similarities of adult and teen. To complete this arrangement, my son and I had to find other accommodations for the weekend. This was a bit of a task for my son. My girls informed my wife of how some of their girlfriends were also sisters to some of my son's friends. Because of this relationship some of the guys also had access and by having access this meant that they, including my son could crash the party. So I spent the next hour or so trying to help my wife figure out which friend of his didn't have a sister and if so how far did any of his friends lived from our house.

So my son was set, with a friend that lived a good distance from our house and I was going over to my cousin's house. It was more of a concern for my wife to allow me to stay over with a relative than for our son to stay with familiar strangers. But she was so excited by the gathering that she would be the one whom the girls would confide. She also figured I couldn't get in that much trouble over two days.

My wife tried to help our son gather his things as if he was going to some camp or something. She tried this same approach with me and after a few looks she backed off. As our son was about to leave, my wife suggested that I should drop him off. The two of us looked at one another as if my wife had gone too far. Yet again I didn't want to spoil her moment so I explained to him he had to ride with me.

Before the two of us could get to the door to leave, my wife again, asked of my assistance. This time it was to help her rearrange the girls' room to now include our niece's bed. So I employed our son and we began to move the dressers from one room to the other so that there were three beds in one room. But that was not enough, my wife wanted the other bed and frame that was in storage that we hadn't decided on if to keep it, bring that up and place that in our daughter's room. As we tried to accomplish this feat, I reminded our son that we would have to do all of this in reverse. He just sighed and pressed me for how long we were to endure. We finally got all the beds in one room when my daughters now wanted to take a stab at home decorating. My son and I probably moved the beds around at least four times before the four of them (wife, girls, and niece) agreed on an arrangement.

After an exhausting and time consuming moment, I left with my son to drop him off at his friends. My wife and the girls met us at the door and all waved, smiled in sort of a unison, which led me to believe that they were up to more than what they let on to me. My son looked back and at them and asked me if we could find a way to snoop on them. I explained the girls would kill him, his mother would punish him, and I would probably have to sleep in his room. I laughed and he didn't find it funny.

I dropped off the fruit of loins and had a brief conversation with his friend's father. The dad was a sort of buffoon, dressed like he was one of the guys and tried to converse with me in slang. I didn't mind the slang, but his gesturing while he spoke, anyway, I prayed to myself that my son would be in good hands, left contact information and tried to be cordial in my attempt to say no to his invitation for men only.

It was good that my Cousin lived around a ½ hour drive away. He lived in a 4 story condominium complex which seemed to indicate an affluent neighborhood. It was a peculiar community that wasn't in proximity of any stores, food or clothing. The mixed community was less active than mine, with less children.

As I pulled into my cousin's driveway, I felt a little unusual. You see, I've spent the night over at my cousin's house, but I haven't stayed over for more than a day. Usually when we realize that it was a timeframe where we had to make a decision either to leave or to stay at the other's place, most of the time either one of us left the other. So staying wasn't a big deal, it just didn't happen often or for long periods. My cousin didn't answer the door right away because he had company. I could hear a pleasant conversation gaining volume as if it was approaching the front door where I stood.

She was...wow and she didn't look like the last girl he had been in a relationship. He introduced her and before I reached out to shake her hand, I'd forgotten her name, habit. She snickered at the both of us and stepped back to give him a big hug goodbye, touched me on the shoulder and left. I stepped out of the doorway just enough to get a view of her and then wondered where she was parked. My cousin looked at me and explained that she was parked in the next door neighbor's driveway, they were out of town and he was watching their place.

As soon as she left, I didn't waste any time inquiring about this latest friend of his and he just laughed at me. I followed him through the vestibule and into his living room before he sat down and explained she was an old friend. I couldn't believe what I was hearing and said to him that I thought he was trying to deceive me. He laughed again countering with his own defense of why can't I of all people believe him and that they were just having some conversation. I told him to explain. He went on to say she came by to have a little fun, but he explained to her that he was changing. He thanked her for asking if he would oblige but since he explained that he couldn't, she accepted...this time. My mouth dropped wide and I kept the pressure on him. He continued with he wasn't quite sure but there was another in his life now and that I'd met her some time ago but they were just pacing themselves to see if they saw their relationship the same way. Once again, my cousin amazed me, but my prejudice fueled my persistence. He again continued with explaining that he and this girl I'd met were taking their time and that she wasn't sure about him. My cousin said that lately some of the girls he'd been meeting didn't move him sexually like this girl and that they have had some in depth conversations. I left the conversation there because...because I knew the girl probably asked him some very personal questions. If he answered the questions he probably did it in vague terms, I was hoping.

We ordered pizza and awaited the delivery while watching some sports channel. Eventually the competition wasn't up to our liking, I dare not say which minimum contact sport we were watching, but the teams…To alleviate our boredom, my cousin suggested we play the video game that he kept around the house for his other "cronies" to play on sports night. So I agreed and he demonstrated the lessons to me and placed the game on beginner level so as to keep his advantage over me to a minimum. Well I'd gotten the hang of the joystick and the buttons and had pretty good hand to eye coordination so I was able to pace him. As my cousin discovered my ability to work the controls of the game, he decided to step up our competition. Our game became more intense, with trash talking, shoving and games of deceit (my cousin "accidentally" pulled the cord to my controller out slightly enough to make the controller react in an erratic form). It took me a while before I figured out how he did it.

Later we talked about the games we played, then it was his buddies that he allowed over to his house, then it was their problems they bring with them on game nights, then it was how each wanted to compare with the other's standing relationship, I had to stop him before I had a cerebral hemorrhage.

This led me back to his friend whom he was trying to have a long standing relationship, and the girl that left. Again he shrugged off the building relationship part and spoke briefly about the girl who left. He explained that they had a standing sexual relationship, it was when either of them was in need and the other would visit. But the girl had started to want more in their "relationship". That's when, he explained that she stalked him, showing up in many places he would frequent after work and then walking down his block one morning. I asked him where he met her. He reluctantly said he met her on one of the lower floors in the corporate building his company was using. He looked at me and I return the stare to which he continued and explained that he thought she could never find him in a building with fifty-three floors of commercial space. He said that his name didn't appear on any directory because he occupied an office slated for someone else that is on long term leave. This added to more confusion and I was getting tired. Tired of his talk, tired of the drinks we kept drinking and physically tired. So I explained I understood his dilemma and started for one of the empty rooms upstairs. My cousin yelled to me that I shouldn't use the second one, but the third because that one was for his new found relationship, that's where she keeps some of her things at times.

I found the sheets and pillow cases and made my bed. I was in the bathroom trying to brush my teeth when there was a knock on the door. It was my cousin and he wanted to talk some more. I already had toothpaste in my mouth and mumbled to him to proceed. I got the real understanding about the girl, who he was leading on and he had been helping her deal with her "appetite", interesting. But when he spoke of this other girl with whom he was getting serious with, first I couldn't believe that there was a chance he was helping her and second, I wanted to meet the one who had the insight to settle the effects of his prison. My cousin told me of how she talked to him as if she had insight into how his prison was affecting him. I didn't change my look of distrust and he brushed it off. He continued with how she could tell that he was hiding secrets, secrets he even kept from himself. I knew then that he would not break to her and started to involve myself in our conversation. My cousin tailed off his explanation as if this is where the two of them had ended and awaits the opportunity to pick up where the two of them left off. I asked him when was the last time he saw her. He said it was a couple of weeks ago. I knew she couldn't handle him and didn't want to deal with his prison and decided to end their little fiasco and letting him down with absence. I gave him some comforting thoughts as he left to do whatever, knowing he would explore the, "What could've been with this girl?" So, I turned out the lights and found the cool part under the sheets.

My dream state would not let me leave alone, the thought of my cousin and this girl. I can picture him going through the same motions as we did as kids and when she was through with him, she would pretend she was in love with him or something. I tossed and turned this dream over and over again in my head. This kept me from sleeping comfortably and it frustrated me. I tossed until I lay in the bed at almost a forty-five degree angle, allowing the toes of my feet to hang over the edge of the bed while I covered my head completely. As I fell in and out of a good sleep, I heard, at least this is what I thought at first, a conversation between my cousin and someone else. Eventually I made it out to be female. The conversation seemed to be directed at me. I wanted to get out of bed, but I decided to lay there so as to let them think I was asleep if they ever came into the room. Well they never came in but they moved about out there beyond my closed door as if they were dancing in a conversation about me.

I remember a similar incident that included my mother in a conversation with my grands about an incident that involved me. I was sent to bed instead of being chastise for an allegation of the sorts. See, I was accused of playing some game with a girl from across the street. Yeah, I did it, but when she was caught, she blamed it all on me. She was caught leaving the porch of my grands when she was told not to cross the street that day. I don't recall why she couldn't cross the street that day. But I was playing with my cousin up and down the street when the girl eventually walked out to her porch steps and sat down to watch us. Well, she had on a skirt and as I walked back and forth past her at times I tried to sneak a peek under her dress. I don't think she knew how to close her legs "lady-like". This continued on a bit until I awakened my prison and it advised me on what I could do to further appease it. So I tried to tempt this girl and coax her into coming over and sitting on the steps of my grand's house. She explained that she couldn't leave her steps and I convinced her that steps are steps and besides, my grand was a very trusting woman in the neighborhood and that her mother looked up to my grandmother with trust. So she checked at her front door to see if anyone would noticed if she'd left her porch, waited for my cousin and the rest of the boys to cross by her and she hurried across the street to the steps of my grands. They boys looked at each other with curiosity about the girl running across the street but continued playing. I paused for a moment to make certain no one gave any thought to her movement.

Well our fun had ended and we all decided to gather at another boy's house, but I had other plans. I convinced my cousin to go ahead without me, stating I had to do a number two and I only wanted to do this in the privacy of my own house. I don't think I expressed it that way to him but that was the outcome. So I made it onto the porch of my grands and there she was waiting patiently for me. We talked about the game I was playing and why we did what did, stuff like that. I eventually convinced her that we should play a game. After all she looked bored sitting on the porch with nothing to do but watch us. She agreed and we played a game I made up that involved peeking with your eyes closed and then guessing what it was with one touch. The game became more elaborate because she involved the furniture, the porch floor, the railing. I grew tired of this and pressed her about herself. She was confused and I explained that we should see if we can tell which body part is which on either one of us. I don't know why she went along but she did, and I had gotten one of my hands up her dress. I think I was supposed to guess the material of her underwear or something. Anyway I wasn't supposed to keep my hand there for such a time and I started to venture inside her underwear. Well at first she didn't stop me and I continued further and further until she became uncomfortable but once again I persisted. With her eyes a bit gazed with confusion and trying to subtly stop me by pushing my hands away, I looked at her with fulfilling a hidden agenda. The girl fidgeted and gasped lightly and I persisted. She made one quick break from me and felt for an itch which was nowhere to be found. She gathered herself and moved to another seat. I sat up and looked over toward her for a while, looking for some sort of response. She couldn't bear to look up at me, but she did ask me why I did what I did to her. I replied to her that I thought that what I did would be something she would like. She said it felt weird but that there was something about it that she feared. I asked her what it was but she couldn't put it into words. She thought that she should leave, I moved over to where she sat and asked her was she mad at me for what I did. She explained no but that she didn't want to do that again at least for some time. I agreed and was relieved that she wasn't upset with me in any way. I knew then that in some way she liked what I did.

So instead we started on some other subject when her cousin had walked by the porch of my grands…the row homes have joined steps which both lead to separate but joined porches and since the neighbor of my grands is enclosed, it can be hard at times to see up onto the porch. The girl's cousin was looking for her. She heard her voice as she was walking by and came up to the porch to inquire. That's when the girl now turned on me because she knew this cousin, who was older would not only tell but interrogate her to find out what was going on between us. The girl started to rant about how I'd tricked her to come up onto the porch of my grands and tried to make her do nasty things. The cousin looked me over and said to me that she knew me because she would see my cousin and me about the neighborhood. The cousin thought I was an innocent kind of kid and moved closer to ask me what happen. I didn't say a thing because around that same time, my grandfather came to the door. He wasn't coming out to see the commotion, but to call my cousin and me into the house for something. He looked at the girl's cousin a bit surprised, made salutations and then asked her why she was up on the porch with the kids. The girl's cousin tried to make it seem to my grand that I was holding the girl hostage and started with the fact that I'd try to pin her down and do things to her and then that's when she heard the sounds from across the street and came over to rescue her from me. My grand looked at me and asked if what the cousin was saying was true, I said no and the cousin tried to reach past my grand to hit me. My grand grabbed her arm and she screamed. My grand looked at her confused and then I could hear from across the street a female and a male voice moving closer to my grand's house. The girl's uncle and mother came over to see what was going on. I could hear kids being alerted of the commotion and running toward my grand's house. After about a few minutes my grand had gained control of the situation. He directed the girl's uncle to tell the kids to move away from the house and not to hang around. My grand instructed the girl's mother and cousin to sit and calm down. That's when he asked the girl if I had done anything to her that she didn't want me to do. The girl said no but she did ask me to stop at one point. Again the cousin got involved shouting epithets, cursing and accusing me of intimidating her cousin to the point where she was afraid to tell the truth. The girl's uncle grabbed the cousin by the arm and escorted her off the porch whereby she started to shout at me. The mother and my grand both agreed on the girl and I being punished separately and we were both instructed to not engage in games together. The mother thanked my grand, snatched up the girl and as they left, she would shake the girl a little then look in her direction with a stern look whispering some things to her. This made the girl cry until she became reluctant to leave, begging for forgiveness and refusing to leave. They eventually left and I could hear the murmuring cry of the girl but I dare not look over the porch railing in her direction. I was afraid of what I was to endure. My grand told me to go in the house and sit in the living room. I did as quickly as I could and sat. Meantime my cousin came in and looked in my direction with the understanding that he was already told not ask me anything. I could hear my cousins and my sisters in the kitchen talking at times about me and at other times, the girl. By now my grand informed me that my mother was on her way. It didn't take long for her to arrive and her and my grands started to discuss the events and my possible punishment. They seemed to not agree and I was sent to bed without dinner. But because I couldn't sleep at such an early time I could hear their conversations. It wasn't clear and I couldn't hear my cousin and sisters. I figured they were told not to come out the kitchen.

When I was eventually let off my punishment my cousin never asked me about that day. At least this is how I will remember it. We sat outside and I looked over across the street at the girl who never looked in my direction. Matter of fact she never spoke to me again and as time passed, so did the moment we shared. It wasn't until my junior high school days that I was able to talk with her. She was cordial and never mentioned that day, but I did and she paused to answer me for effect and lit into me about how I tricked her into sex and how I lied to my grand, her mother, uncle and cousin. I tried to defend myself but it was no good. The girl made up her mind that day because of the embarrassment, chastisement and that she didn't know what we were really doing. I tried to explain and apologize. She waved in my direction and walked away. My cousin told me later that she was always a bit reserved about talking with guys and that she had a little mean streak in her but he didn't know why. My cousin defended what he said early that the girl seemed bitter. I said I wish I hadn't met her.

It was weird, but I would see this girl on more than one occasion. As I've looked back on this moment, I've drawn the conclusion that our meeting was to add healing for this girl. I didn't know how much our encounter had an effect on her and it was my fault. I wanted to remove that scar for her and at the same time find some redemption for myself, if she would give it to me. I would meet her again later in life, she was fifteen and I...I was just turning thirteen and not even in high school, older women?

I did see her again, when we were a little older, some time when we were in college and I was visiting my grands. I was at the corner store when I saw her passing by through the window. I quickly paid for my purchase, stepped outside and ran in her direction. When I finally caught up to her I made salutations and she reluctantly returned the same.

When we met then she explained to me how much that moment hurt her. It was not our moment, but the fact we had gotten caught that hurt her. She explained that she came over because she had a liking for me and that because she couldn't come off the steps, many of the other boys didn't speak to her. She went on to say that this distance she got from the boys transcended into school, where it was pretty much known that if one was to hold a conversation with her, it had to be from the confines of her steps. I tried to get in a word, but she continued more with how crazy her mother would get if she asked to go outside. This mannerism was less but still present when she did have girlfriends over. She said it took her mother some time to eventually give her some space to roam the neighborhood. But when that happened I was visiting less to my grands. She looked at me with a thought, and then asked if I ever thought that her mother was still watching me as I grew to be certain of my actions? I apologized again, but she wouldn't accept my apology because our moment kept her fearful of guys. She started to tell me how she wanted that day to have never have happen and that she felt betrayed because how she felt about me. She went on to say when guys try to hold a conversation with her; she is always listening for the persuasion from them. This is why she can't trust men…period. Then I could see the tears welling in her eyes, and she looked away for a moment. About this time a few people walking past were looking on with curiosity. She gathered herself and said she wishes she could trust because she does like men. I thought for a moment why a guy wouldn't speak to her? After all she is attractive. I carefully reached out to her, she drew her hand away, and I knew it was me that gave her the fear. I didn't move but in my most calming voice, I started to say she was right and that I had seen this act by other guys in the neighborhood so I thought it was the thing to do. She looked at me as if I wasn't there and countered with an analogy that is someone did this, would I be so inclined to do the same? I answered yes, yes because I was young and impressionable but that doesn't excuse my behavior. I kept trying to apologize and she asked me if my apologizing was to remove a burden of guilt off my shoulders? I said initially yes, but after what she explained to me, I felt I needed to find a way to help her come to terms and find peace even if she never forgave me. She paused and thought about what I just said. She said she would give it some thought. That would be the last I would see her but I could see that she was relieved that we had spoken, that I wanted to admit my lies and deceit and wished her happiness and healing. We finally said our goodbyes on better terms and she continued down the street. I watched her as she never looked back. She did however, crossed the street. That's when I knew she wanted to look back to see if I was looking at her or if I'd left. She never looked in my direction but I stared in her direction until she turned the corner. It wasn't until recently that her scares from that day started to heal…I'm hoping.

Speculation

My son approached me first with the idea of his going out with a few of his friends to a neighbor's house around the corner for an evening pool party. He was standing in front of me with his towel, shower shoes, goggles, a sleeveless shirt and long leg trunks. Initially I stared at him curiously with one eyebrow raised. Somewhere in his asking there was something else that was to occur at this party. I looked at him with a questioning gesture. He pleaded with me, citing all the concerns I normally would ask him and all the precautions he would have to carry out. I gave him my blessing to attend and before I could finish, the knock at the door was for him. After he had opened the door, his buddies walked in to inform him how they too had enacted the same response from their parents. My son gave them the indication that I was eavesdropping, they looked past him startled and then they all made loud emphatic salutations towards me. I never gave my son the concerned look and he was off before I could give him a time to return.

After they had left, sometime later, my daughters and my niece comes into the kitchen where I was foraging through the refrigerator. They verbally played around with me about the notion of this big party and how all the kids will be there and how there would be chaperones there and all this food was there and so on. I tried to listen and kept wondering where my wife was at the moment. My youngest explained that they had spoken with their mother earlier in the day and that she said if I agreed, then they could go to the party. So I played along with their game a little until my eldest comes over and sits beside me to explain that my niece has not been to a pool party before since she had been staying with us. At first I wasn't moved, but reconsidered because the night was warm but not hot and their brother was there. They didn't know this part of the circumstances and I conceded quickly without a fuss.

They too were already dressed for the party. They all had on bikinis with wild patterns and various colors with shorts over top and "flip-flops". Of course the shorts my niece was wearing were on the snug side and seem to be a little lower than the types my daughters were wearing. She was in fact more developed than my girls. She looked "different" than she did when she was wearing her pants at the miniature golf that night. Those three could not stop talking as they made their way to the front door. I could still hear them as they walked down the pathway.

As I started to relax, I heard a knock at the door and some ruffling of bags. Then I heard a rampant knock and loud thuds of some sort. By the time I opened the door, my wife was doing some sort of bent knee, cross your legs, hop around dance and she held up her index finger for me to pause. For some reason she couldn't talk and I just waited. When she finally gathered her composure, I stepped to the side and she scurried past me to the bathroom near the kitchen. I stepped out onto the door step and gathered the many bags she brought home.

While she prepared to exit the bathroom I inquired about the bags and the fact that she was almost to the brink of wetting herself. She laughed and explained that she thought she could make it home, and she did, but she had forgotten about getting the bags out of the car. She went on to say that she wasn't sure if I had stepped out for a moment or was busy doing something. I laughed at her and she knew why and lightly slapped me up side my head.

Later she asked me about the kids and I explained how she set me up and so on. She asked about the whereabouts of our son and again I explained he too set me up. I felt a little naïve about how I was set up, but it made her laugh. When she finished, she led me into a conversation of how the kids were growing and soon the house would be empty and at that time the house would be too big for the two of us. I countered with how close we were to paying off the mortgage and that we should look forward to having space if one of them happens to return or for the grandkids. She felt comforted by my sincerity that I didn't want to move anywhere. There is so much you have to plan and moving should only occur if there are some mitigating circumstances. Besides, the children grew up in this house.

I sat in the chair with the ottoman and my wife crossed her legs and laid sideways on the couch as we watched, what I call a woman's show. She occasionally changed the stations and looked over to see if I would react. Nothing. I was enjoying the quiet atmosphere throughout the house. It was surreal how for this moment we had nothing we needed to do, nothing was pending and we could do whatever we wanted. I was taken how this was a moment that would resemble my later life. It could wear on you quickly.

But I couldn't stop thinking about the house. We were so proud when we purchased it. The price was within our budget and the neighborhood was full of various families in age, backgrounds. It was a welcoming sight for us. The neighbors called us the "teeny-boppers" because they thought we the youngest couple. Yes we were young, newlyweds, with ambition and a long "honey-do" list.

…We were excited to know that we would soon be moving into a house instead of having to continue living in the apartment that my mother rented for all of us. The house was at the other end of the city and it was in an area we hadn't heard much about. My sisters and I tried to find out the location of the house by asking our grandparents, but they could vaguely recall any landmarks that would help us. Someone in my family mentioned that we should ask our aunt who might have and idea of the location. In this area of understanding, she was useless. I'd discovered on that day that I had been to more areas of the city than she, but I never told a soul.

After finding out that we were moving, our cousins acted in a way that seemed as if they were upset with something. My younger sister mentioned that they were jealous of our being able to move. Now as an adult, I understood their displeasure with what was happening to us. But then, I felt betrayed that they would feel this way toward us. For a few days, or maybe weeks, my cousin and I played sparingly with one another.

After several months and settling into the house and neighborhood, my sisters and I started to slowly venture further out with our new found friends. My sisters had their friends and I had mine. However, many of our friends were friends and that made relationships easy.

I was on my own, per se, and took pleasure in every new experience. I was quite comfortable in my new setting and enjoyed it immensely. So much that I found what I called at the time, a girlfriend. To me she was a girlfriend, but to adults, she was puppy love. Nonetheless, I really liked her. I had asked her one day if I could, as we would say in those days, "stand a chance with her", and she replied yes. Without hesitation, she replied yes. From that point forward in my mind we were a couple. As a couple we were supposed to do things together. Like, when I would share all my treats with her and even played with her toys (dolls mainly) when no one was around. Every moment I could spend with her I could.

It wasn't until one day at dusk when my prison came alive. For quite some time it had laid dormant and at times I hadn't given it any thought or reason to surface. My prison had the same drive it had that day with the other girl who earlier had accepted my apology. I didn't want it to take over me, not with my girlfriend. She was even more special to me than the other girl. We had something between us.

It started when my new girlfriend and I began talking about "those things" that grownups did in the privacy of their rooms or otherwise. I don't remember how the subject started, but I do remember the content. The conversation explored the very details which I was privy, but I tried not to let on that I had knowledge. She trusted my judgment and assumed that I would have more information than she. For some strange reason she assumed that I had experience. As the conversation delved deeper, I became more excited in the thought that we could indulge ourselves in the very subject and I could show her.

Eventually she conceded to my persuasion of attempting to replicate what adults do in those circumstances. Again, I've always hated myself for moments in my past like this one. As I had slowly but surely assured her that we would be okay in our indulgence, I also informed her that I wouldn't tell. She assured me that she too would do the same. I then told her that this act that we were about to embark would be special to only us. This act would link us together forever. She acknowledged my assurance.

To this day I can't put all the moments together sequentially, but I do remember having my girlfriend in a particular position whereby we were both laying on our sides and I laid behind her. At this point, her shorts were down and I was working on her panties. I, without her knowing, had already gotten my pants open and my boyhood out of my underwear from the side. Nothing happened initially until she became nervous about our actions. I leaned up over her and peered over her to inquire her uneasiness. She explained how nervous she was doing this and kept questioning me if this endeavor would hurt. I couldn't give her the answer of "yes", because I didn't know. As I moved closer behind her, she started to whimper out of concern and I tried to calm her down. Her whimper became a light cry and then a low wail. She started to slowly panic and began to tremble a little. These actions lead to her whaling out loud. I panicked and started to yell at her to be quiet. She tried for a moment and slowly began her escapade again.

Eventually I moved away from her, redressed (fixed my underwear and pulled up my pants) and started helping her dress. All the while I kept assuring her that everything was going to be okay. She explained through her running tears and nasty running noise that she thought she was pregnant from this experience. I had never heard this and started thinking the same. I begged her not to tell and that I would find a solution. She tried to listen to me through her sniffling. Finally she stopped crying and as we tried to leave the narrow alcove on the backside of a house down the street from hers, a friend of my girlfriend's heard the crying. This girl didn't like me very much and started to yell for attention once she saw us walking together.

As I ran down the street away from them, this older boy in the neighborhood caught up to me and grabbed me by the arm. He began rapidly questioning me and I couldn't put my sentences together. This boy started to pull me back to where I left my girlfriend and I tried to resist. He was stronger than I but his grip was gentle. I think he was on my side but wanted to put end to this moment.

As the stories unfolded, my girlfriend and I could not collaborate. It was deduced by our parents that we were doing something more than what we led them to believe. In front of the forming crowd of children, I was chastised by my mother with a belt. What saved me were the blue jeans I was wearing, but my arms took a lashing. I tried desperately not to scream from the pain. Because I showed no signs of breaking, my mother continued with all her might. Eventually the uncomfortable pain started to rise within me. The more I cried, the more it seemed my mother tore into my hide. At one point I thought I had started to become numb to the lashings because I could not feel them, however, it looked as if my mother was swinging double time. My now ex-girlfriend was slapped a couple of times on her bottom while her mother held one of her arms. She danced around for a moment, then she began to cry softly. It was more embarrassment for her than anything else. Meantime, after my mother finished with me, she made me apologize. I walked up to my girlfriend who didn't want to look at me and I started to apologize. When I was almost finished, she glanced at me with shame. I felt betrayed that she didn't accept my apology. My mother apologized to my ex-girlfriend's mother only to arrange a meeting later, and sent me along to walk home humiliated. With some distance between me and my mother, who stood in place to continue talking with my ex-girlfriend's mother, the other neighborhood kids began to heckle me. Some shoved me around and others poked me with their index fingers. My ex-girlfriend's nosey friend was in on the taunts and even threatened me not to even look her way or my ex-girlfriend's direction again. I was never scared of her, but I knew if I beat on her, I probably wouldn't be able to tell this story.

Once again I had lost a friend, but this time, this one was forever. I never had the opportunity to explain my side nor if I did I don't think it would've lessen my punishments. My ex was a willing victim and became scared at the unknown, but I did not set out to harm her…only, indirectly, infect her? I was told by my mother not to speak to my ex, look her way and if I had to walk home, and she was on the same side of the street, I was to take another street. My punishment was simple for this incident; stay in my room all day with no television or toys or direct contact with the members of our household. When it was time to eat, I ate by myself downstairs alone. I almost thought I was living alone because at one point, I hadn't seen my sisters for about three or four days.

But because this was the summer and my mother suspected this entire incident would pass by the time school would start, she decided to send me to my grandparent's to spend the rest of the summer. At first I thought I could spend more time with my cousin outside, but then I was informed that I had to get permission first from my "grands". Often times they were more ruthless mentally in their objective to have you learn your lesson than my mother. I thought that notion would blow over after being there awhile until it hit me…I would see her! I conjured up in my mind this moment of realization that places you in awe. My life was going well, but now…it was like a heavy boulder was placed over my little chest and every which way I turned, the pain worsened.

The rest of that summer was…well…like a living nightmare with moments filled with contradictions regarding my actions. I didn't know if I was coming or going before and after each episode. Over my "grands" I stayed in more trouble that summer than I like to call "petty" in terms of offenses. In addition, this time I could not save my cousin.

My son came in the house in an uncaring manner, alerted his mother and me of his presence and proceeded to ascend the stairs. Before he could reach the second step, my wife had called him back to interrogate him. He danced around the events that took place at the pool party and denied any involvement in anything. By acting in this manner, he sparked our curiosity as to what really occurred at the pool. My wife dug deeper into his story and our son faltered again with his story. This led us to put on some presentable clothes and escort him back to the party.

When we arrived, most of the commotion had subsided and many of the kids were breaking off into their own little groups. We passed by my daughters who didn't want to make eye contact but my niece was nowhere to be found. We made salutations to our neighbors who owned the house and tried to discuss the events. We were lucky, we were the first parents to arrive. They were very cordial in their explanation to us about how they pieced together the events.

What we discovered was initially my son and his friends were dancing with the girls a little close. The girls in turn, were reciprocating with some sultry movements and then the party slowly got out of hand. One girl in particular was the center of attraction for some of the boys. At that point, some of the girls became jealous. Then some of the boys began feeling, grabbing and touching areas of the bodies of many of the girls. Finally one of the girls got upset. This somehow led to a girl's bikini bottom being ripped at the strings on one side by one of the boys. The girl was able to cover up, but a great deal was seen by all. My son was the culprit part of the group; the group of jealous girls included my daughters and the victim…my niece.

Once we got all the information, we looked toward our children. Some of the kids waited in excitement to see if we were going to chastise them publicly. This was not going to occur. Instead we whispered some instructions to each of them without giving any indication that they were headed for trouble. We concluded our visit by thanking the other parents, excusing ourselves and waiting by the gate for our children to say their "goodbyes" for the night.

The walk home was long and quiet with the kids in front and me and my wife in the rear. There were the occasional whispers and the slight pointing of fingers but overall the kids remained civil. My son remained silent, never looking in anyone's direction but forward and didn't waver in his walk. However, the walk took a turn for worst when my niece wanted to switch her hands to continue holding her shorts up over her ripped bikini. I had almost forgotten about the girls wearing shorts out of the house. My wife stopped to help her as she became upset. She was acting agitated, pulling, and twitching with each try to somehow hold the bikini together under her shorts. I moved to join other the kids and at first we waited for them to catch up, then we walked on, slowly. When my wife and niece had caught up to our pace, my wife motioned for me to again step to the rear. Unfortunately, what my wife had done for our niece didn't help much, but my wife informed her that it was dark, a lot of what was showing on our niece could not be seen and we were almost home.

As we continued home, my niece tried to rest her other hand and at times just simply removed her hand from her shorts and allowed the damaged side of the bikini to fall. My wife spoke softly and with a steady voice of encouragement because my niece displayed her disgust in her own effort. But in her effort she inadvertently exposed the top portion of her rear. This occurred this one time and unfortunately I was able to have a glance. I had a firsthand look and tried in many ways to look away. I could feel my wife's stare to remind me of my duty as an adult and a surrogate parent. But my niece, somehow, she knew. I'm not sure if it was the fact that she walked second from the end on my side, or that she was becoming more comfortable during this walk, but she turned this once to say something to my youngest daughter when our eyes met. I think she was making an effort to make sure she was letting me know that she saw me.

I was becoming infatuated with what I was seeing which was actually nothing, but when my wife nudged me and with a gesture of disapproval, she pointed slightly in the direction of our niece. She whispered to me that she was going to sit down with her privately and talk to her about being a lady and what not to wear in public. She was growing tired of reminding our niece to be mindful of her broken bikini string under her now loose fitting shorts. I somewhat ignored my wife and continued to find alternatives to looking in my niece's direction.

Eventually, the mood I was trying to feel wore off because guilt filled me. It was because I tried to use this moment to prepare my infection for my niece and this notion took me back to many of my previous experiences with all the repercussions I had endured. I hadn't felt that way in a long time and vowed not to experience that emotional ride again, but right now the feeling was there somewhere in my gut. Unfortunately once I started on this path I could not find a way or method to turn it off. As we continued to walk I fidgeted, or at least I thought this emotional feeling was an outward expression. My self infliction tormented me at this moment to do something or to at the very least prepare to implement this infection. This moment of emotion gave me reason, an excuse, in finding ways in which to separate my niece from the rest of my family where we could be alone. During this moment of convincing, I entertained the thought process of how I could actually get away with doing something like this to my niece. But as I continued to think, process the events in sequential order, a sickness again convicted me of my past and those that were possibly infected if not were for some interference. As I continued to chastise myself, I could feel my brow contorting into deep crevices above my eyes. The effect was a portrayal of deep concentration and internal thought. In the meantime this action caused me to stiffen in my facial expression. That's when the pain of holding this physical appearance started to take hold and I realized that there was a possibility that my wife would notice this entire transformation. I internally fought this off and hoped that no one, especially my wife, noticed my uneasiness. As I begin to gain some control, I felt some sort of hot flash through my body and in an instant it was fleeting. I felt I should hold on to this because it felt alive in me. But alas for the moment I was free and tried not to entertain my prison.

Transition

In the hours that followed after my niece and my kids decided to bring embarrassment to us all, the house took on a different presence. Everyone seemed distant and reluctant to truly interact as we once did. I understood that the kids were afraid of any form of chastisement and the embarrassment of the whole thing. But I did not want to exist in a home where there is an unspoken word of implied actions. It would seem as if we were passing ships on the sea, passing by with no acknowledgement of the other and knowing that the other was there.

My wife finally inquired if I had a conversation with our son about the incident and I explained that we had a brief conversation but nothing in detail. My wife exploded, accusing me of cowardice and pampering our son because I would become afraid if he started to dislike me after I questioned his motive in the incident. I tried to defend myself countering her accusation with worthless details as to the why and how I didn't speak in more detail with our son. She began to laugh as I continued with my discussion hoping that the more I spoke, the more I became convincing to her. The likewise was becoming more evident to me and she knew it. I conceded to her push and want to redirect my emotion of being caught and feeling unpleasant onto my son.

As I arrived to his door, a side of me was hoping that this entire event was just about boys testing their wills and what they thought they could get away with. I entered my son's room again after a brief knock. He did not anticipate the visitor at his door was going to be, again. I explained to him that there was more about this incident that I needed to have him explain to me. I told him he had to make me free comfortable with what had happened this evening. As my son began to plead his case I realized that in his blabbering he was exploring, but he was disrespectful in his approach. First, I put an end to his talking by holding up my index finger in the air to stop him. He didn't, and I cut the space between us in more than a half and gave him a look that indicated that I had had enough and if he didn't stop...he stopped as I closed the distance between us. I began to explain to him that he shouldn't succumb to pressures from his friends like that and to follow his true heart when it comes to girls. My son explained that his cousin was the most endowed and that she had a way about her that was enticing. My son went on to say some of the other boys were interested in his sisters but his cousin was the one they conjured lies about and the stories were endless. I began to explain to him that the both of them were too young to embark upon something that required a more mature understanding, besides this was his cousin. This is something that is not done. For a moment he seemed to show that he didn't care but I waited on his response. He finally tried again to justify his actions by explaining that he wouldn't have gone as far as he did if the other boys didn't push him into to doing it. He explained further that they convinced him that this was just his cousin and if he hadn't seen his cousin yet then he wouldn't understand. My son continued by saying that he thought it was alright because he recalled the days when they were younger. I felt a huge something like a gigantic burp or something developing in my chest. I started to reflect on the subject of my wife and me and even the other parents skewing the perceptions of our children with too much association growing up. My son waited for my response. By now he was convinced that there wasn't going to be some sort of beating on my second trip to his room. I began slowly to explain in great detail the reasons why he shouldn't consider his cousin nor should he consider going as far as he did with some other girl in the manner that he did. To add I explained that he had ample time to explore girls and that he should try to become friends with a female and then, and only then...I couldn't end up at the same subject I was trying to convince him to avoid. This was where we almost started, so I tailed off my conversation and ended it with this matter involves his cousin. He looked at me as if he understood and I left him hanging on that last note.

In the days that followed, I noticed how everyone continued to avoid one another as if each had the plague or something. This avoidance agitated me to my wits end and in my conversations that followed I spoke with an aggressive manner. Because of my agitated manner, my girls tried to avoid me with short quick responses, while my niece never came out of her room when I was present. My wife ignored me and even got a laugh out of my actions as she moved in and out of conversations with me. But my son continued to believe that my actions were an end result of my not chastising him from our last encounter. He often looked in my direction like scared prey who tried to act as if they were not moved by the present circumstances or the possibility of what was to come. So instead he would cower in my presence, say what he had to say and move on. Oftentimes he'd glance back to check that all was well and accepted of his reverence to me.

This avoidance led me to consider my cousin in his actions as I discovered his first infection. That summer had already become a sour one for me because I was sent to my "grands" as punishment. I had just arrived, greeted everyone that I laid eyes on, and found my way upstairs to my room…rather my cousin's room. As I started to unpack, my cousin entered the room we shared and we greeted each other with a familiar handshake and hug. My cousin was elated to see me and wanted to inform me of all the fighting, courtships, thievery and problems that plague other families in the neighborhood.

I took it all in as fast as I could and as we began to leave the upstairs to find our way somewhere out in the streets, my grandfather stood at the porch stairs outside waiting on us. We were so shocked at his presence that we stopped conversing and started looking arbitrarily in directions other than each other. My grandfather called me closer to him and instructed my cousin to go on off the porch and find something to do. I stood there knowing in some way that I was to be punished again for the incident back home. My grandfather stood over me and waited for my eyes to connect with his. It took awhile before I could muster up enough bravery to do so. When I did he began slowly to explain to me that he was disappointed with my actions and if I thought about doing something similar like that here that he would basically "skin" me alive with a beating. He further asked me if I understood what he was saying, I responded and he turned to walk back into the house.

Just before he began to ascend the steps to the house, he turned and looked at me again. I hadn't moved yet and he reminded me that I couldn't go out until my mother said that it was okay. So after my grandfather disappeared, I walked back into the house, made my way back upstairs to the room that I shared with my cousin, laid in the bed and counted the shapes in the repetitious wallpaper until sleep became my friend.

Something finally awoke me. There was the now famous moaning that I had grown accustom to hearing from my aunt, but it was faint. I sat up thinking I was having a dream. That was not the answer and I looked about the room until I was almost dizzy. At this moment I did not recognize that I was sweating a little from my sleep and from the unknowing that I was experiencing. But what made my panic real was that I was in a darkened room due to the sun setting and I hadn't turned on the lights. I heard it again and this time it was consistent. It even seems closer than when I first heard it. I did not know where to start my search, so as I quietly turned on the lights to my bedroom hoping that this was not happening in my room, I could hear the moans more distinctly. As I started to open the bedroom door, it creaked and it was just about that time the moaning stop. As I entered the hallway I paused to listen about the hallway all the while searching with my eyes as if the sound would appear as something. I didn't know which way to turn to search first, but I tried to recall in which direction I heard the moaning. Fortunate for me I turned left and walked done the long hallway to further investigate the sound. Now I was at the end of the hallway. From behind I heard movement and slowly turned, preparing myself for some sort of scare. It never came, but my cousin did. He moved assuredly and as he approached me, he inquired how long had I been up from my nap. I tried to answer without letting him know that I had heard my familiar sounds, the sounds from aunt. He looked me over to determine if I was guilty of noticing anything. I tried to appear innocent of knowing anything, besides I wasn't sure what to be guilty of.

That's when my cousin just turned and walked away from

me. I rushed to catch him and when I grabbed him by his arm, just about the bicep, I realize that he was actually in a stupor. As I have replayed this scene over in my mind, and as I've grown, I have come to realize that this was his behavior. It was the same type of behavior that I experienced the first couple of times with my aunt. But at the time I assumed he was trying to ignore me or give me some sort of hint through his ignoring me. I pressed him into telling me what was the problem and he began to become very defensive. He was so defensive that we argued over my snooping on him. She accused me of hiding things from him since I arrived. The bombardment of questions and accusations made me angry. So angry that before I could push him away from me he began shoving me. Then we began a shoving match which then he took a swing at me that made me jump backwards. Just then my cousin began swinging repeatedly and at the same time rushing toward me. His punches were all over the place. I tried to block as many punches as I could, but some landed and others hung in the air. Eventually my cousin had backed me onto one side of the hallway, buried his head into my midsection and continued to swing. I could hear softly his unsettling whimper, but I had to defend myself. So I began throwing my own punches, uppercuts. My cousin's head began to bobble from the hits and then he stepped back with more determination to assault me. He leaned in again and threw an over handed left hook. It cracked my jaw and pain shot up into my head. I flinched with pain and grimaced. As my cousin regrouped to throw more punches, I waited for him to lunge in at me. I held up a knee to give pause to his action, stepped toward him and tried to plant myself in a position to retaliate. That's when he paused long enough for me to begin, my own barrage of punches. My cousin stammered backwards and slammed back first up against the wall. As I continued my punching, he threw out a flailing kick which hit me almost squarely in my groin. I stumbled forward and then he grabbed me. By now my legs have given way and I could feel them buckling underneath me. I held onto him for bracing until I could gather my composure, but he spun me around and grabbed my right hand tightly and began to twist it by looping himself under my arm. Once he had a twist on me, he just held me in place and looked at me. I eventually fell to my knees from both the twisting pain and the pain I was recovering from between my legs. I leaned over with my free arm and held my other arm in pain. I didn't know which pain to address because the pain from two different areas caused some tearing in my eyes. I looked in my cousin's direction and begged for release. My cousin looked back at me with sorrow in his eyes as if I had, or someone had, betrayed him. I couldn't speak anymore for the pain and just waved my other hand in the air to signify submission, but he still wouldn't let go of his grip. Now I started cry tears of pain and tried again to speak something, but my mouth had accumulated too much saliva. I was drooling and didn't even know it. I squint my eyes to absorb the pain because it felt like it was shooting directly into my brain. I lay in place frozen unable to look back at him any longer. I could feel my cousin slowly releasing his grip but not my hand. I nodded in gratitude, and my cousin eventually released my hand. The pain was so excruciating that I let go of my own body control and of my arm only to allow myself to just fall where it may. I hit the floor in a thud and just laid there quietly sobbing some and hoping the pain would subside. I couldn't twist myself over because I was wedged in the floor with my own weight on my good shoulder.

I could hear my cousin in the distance because the pain held my eyes shut; he was still standing near or in front of me. As I tried to reflect back on this moment, it appeared that my cousin was admiring his quick work of me because he stood in place somewhere off in the distance. I could hear his breathing. Eventually the pain ceased enough where I could lift myself up and then lay comfortably on the floor. My cousin waited for me to gather my faculties and slowly moved toward me. I was starting to lift myself up in order to sit upright. I began to flinch, thinking he was about to attack me again. Instead he stood on the other side of the hallway against the wall and slowly slid down until he sat staring at me from across the space. I said nothing because I did not know what to expect next. Everything around us seemed to stand still as we occasionally glanced at one another and then about the hallway.

Eventually he began to speak, or mumble, but it was in such a low tone that I had to beg him to speak louder or come closer. He refused to the latter and began to speak in a louder voice. But as he started, he stopped and grabbed his mouth with both hands. He looked as if he were two people, one who wanted to speak and the other, someone or something that wanted to hold him hostage for fear of what he was about to tell me. His eyes widened in a look of panic.

I knew then that there was some sort of secret involved in this discussion and I wanted to be a part of this conspiracy. So, I moved slowly across the hallway to be near him. My cousin looked downward in guilt and wanted to ask me if what he had done was wrong. I didn't know how to answer him, so I questioned him more about the subject, to figure out what was the trouble. He looked at me as if I had already known the subject. He became hesitant at that point because he was accusing me as to my knowledge of the subject. My cousin looked away as if in shame and started to lean his head back against the wall. I moved closer, extended my arm and tried to calm him down by tapping him on his shoulder. He pulled away from me with the attitude that I was showing him cynicism instead of empathy.

He sighed at first then looked downward before telling me his story. My cousin started off slow and the anticipation grew inside me to the point where I became fidgety. My cousin looked over toward me to inquire but ignored my movements. His story unfolded before my eyes! It was if I was back at that moment when our aunt first approached me. My cousin cried as if he had done some unspeakable crime, punishable by death. He explained how our aunt had been trying to lure him into her bedroom to play games but he didn't like playing with her all that much. He continued with how he went to the bathroom to brush his teeth when he opened the door and found our aunt standing with one leg up on the side of the tub with her back to the door. She was in her long house coat and it looked as if she didn't have anything on underneath. My cousin said that because she was in the bathroom already that he knew he should have left. He said he didn't know what she was doing but she was preoccupied such that she almost didn't hear him enter. Our aunt didn't yell at him, but explained he would have to pay for this infraction. She then allowed him to stay in the bathroom with her to brush his teeth. He was so nervous that he dropped the toothbrush on the bathroom floor, then later in the sink and just fumbled with holding it. He said she continued her efforts without missing a beat and that's when he turned to see what she doing, she was methodically clipping the hairs from her precious. When she looked up and caught him staring, she just smiled and told him to finish because they had to deal with his unannounced entry.

Later, a few days later, this is when he tells me that I had not arrived just yet, that our aunt called him upstairs and into her room. In the sketchy details he explained, he describes her playing with his manhood and having him do the same with her precious. This took a while until she directed him to accompany her on her bed. This is where she tried to sit on him but her weight wasn't right and it bothered him. He said he asked if he could leave and she explained that this was the only way she wouldn't tell our grands.

His telling of the story at this point was broken, missing continuity, always reflecting on more than one part or subject and I was getting lost. In frustration my cousin said that she smelled flowery over her body, but he could smell a sweat like odor coming up from the floor where he stood over her. For the dumbest reason I still cannot explain, I asked him if he smelled tomatoes at that point. He looked at me asking why he would smell tomatoes.

We sat there with our backs pressed up against the wall looking into space not knowing what the next thing to talk about was. That's when we heard our aunt coming upstairs. She ascended the steps without a care or concern in the world. When she reached the second floor, she spoke to the both of us and smiled. My cousin couldn't look in her direction and instead occupied the moment with staring into the floor. I never looked away, I kept my eyes on her and wanted her to see the expression on my face of resentment, shame, disgust, anger and revenge. She paused before turning toward the direction of her room door and looked back to us. She said that later on, maybe after dinner or on another day the three of us can "play" together with no interruptions. Neither one of spoke, but I could tell my cousin was processing the term "play", and he moved a little closer to me. My eyes never left the sight of her. I was so enraged at her for what she did to him. I felt I needed to take some sort of act of revenge but didn't know how. I sat there looking in her direction until she closed the door behind her and tried with all my heart to devise a plan. While I thought about my plan I heard my cousin mention that we were going to get it. I ignored his whimpering statement and wanted to try to convince him that we had to work together in order to defeat her. In my mind, I can still remember what I said back then, if my cousin wouldn't help me defeat her then I would have to do the work myself. At that moment I had never felt a need to cause such harm, not kill, but long suffering harm. As we sat there I tried not to let my cousin hear the gnashing of my teeth.

From that moment forward if anything happened to one or the other (my cousin and I), we almost couldn't tell because of how we became accustom to the endeavor. Our effort became a second nature of endurance. We went through with what we had to endure with our aunt, felt badly in the process, felt anger afterwards, tried to develop a plan of punishment for her and eventually went on about our regular day. To do this on a regular basis meant that we could no longer find our way out of this mess. Besides we only had each other to turn to for help. On some occasions when I did see my cousin at my grands, I could tell "she" had already had her way with him. Likewise, after my experience, my cousin could tell the same about me. After each moment, we would leave the other be for a moment and then hold a soft conversation to get the other to not become upset and to try to ignore the matter altogether. That was one of the hardest things we had to tell each other. But my pain subsided over time because I didn't' have to endure our aunt's advances as much as he did. So, my healing came faster than for my cousin.

However, my cousin was slowly changing into a person of no regard to himself or others. He wasn't reckless, but I still to this day can't place a verb to it, but I know that he would never be the same person. On occasion he would do something he wasn't suppose to do and when he was caught, he would admit to it and just take on the chastisement. Our grands often wondered why after he did something he just didn't care if he was caught. He was not a person looking for trouble nor was he one who would cause trouble; he would just get into trouble by himself and await the punishment. I tried when I could to offset his punishment by lying and saying that it was me who did the deed. This lying only got me an additional beating along with the one that was sometime believed for me. On the other side of those moments, I would try to stop my cousin before he did his deed only to be caught "red-handed" as if I was the one who actually did the deed. After our fiasco of jumping around, ducking and yes, screaming, we were sent to the room we share. There we would console each other ending with my cousin thanking me once more and my questioning him why he did what he did. He would shrug his shoulders, shake his head and throw his hands up as if he was just giving up.

In the days or weeks that followed, he would ask about me often when I was at home. He begged to be allowed to visit me and/or spend the night over. But for whatever reason he was never allowed. Even to this day I try to come up with a reason for that gesture. But as soon as I arrived he would be so happy and then we would have to go into the mode of protecting one another. Eventually I took most of the assaults from our aunt when I visited. My cousin thanked me for stepping in for him but the fact that I went through it wouldn't satisfy neither of us. The interaction with our aunt occurred anyway whether it was him or I and when that stopped would we be relieved. So when I arrived, he clung to me as if he wasn't sure the truth would get out and we both would be discovered this time. We comforted each other in our secret,

"…let's play?"

encouraging the other to be strong and not to give into telling. But the moments kept coming and we both grew weary that this would never end. I knew that if this, this thing act of ours would ever get out we would be in great trouble. If it did, I knew that I could handle whatever was to come of it, but I wasn't too sure about my cousin. This I still believe he would never be able to endure alone.

Dispossession

"…let's play?"

I never meant to hurt my nephew, in fact I was so proud to be notified of his birth. You see, it meant I was not the youngest at the family gatherings any longer. Even if it meant he was the one to be pampered, I could not stand the attention I got just because of the position I held. It was sickening to hear my family acknowledge me as if they had to alert the other members of my presence. You could always hear, "…oh, oh, here's she comes…look at her!"

My parents often referred to me as the one who could do no wrong. My sisters lightly fought over who could possess me if for only a moment. To them, I came to realize in my reflection, I was the new baby doll. My dad would just pick me up, hug me, look deep into my eyes and smile with pride. You know, that's all he really did, pick me up, hug me, smile in my face and tell me how beautiful I was. This was what I heard growing up. My mother was a bit reserved in how she dealt with me. She was my "teach" early on. She taught me how when I sat, how to sit. You know the things we females explain to our newest sister in life. My mother spoke to me in a calm voice and was never quick to correct me. This application of her upbringing of me never sat well with my sisters. They would remind me since those days of how things were with them when they were growing up. I could only imagine how these two people, our parents, could be so cruel at times. Because of this action, my parents and my sisters would often speak of me in terms of being an object. They approached me making certain that I was never aware of the true things that made up my family. In general conversation, no one really wanted to know what I thought. I just had to play stupid and speak in an imaginative tone with bewilderment in my eyes as if the actual world never existed and I could live in this fantasy palace of a home for ever, bullshit.

As my nephew started to grow up, he grew so fast; he looked up to me for guidance when I was around. Everyone loved how he became my shadow. When I wasn't around, he would look for me, become a little sadden when I left, oftentimes, he'd cry. It was I who secretly showed him how to stand before he began to walk. I knew he was becoming frustrated when it was time for me to move somewhere else in the house. Besides he was starting to become heavy. I couldn't keep picking him up, I couldn't lift him anymore.

Oftentimes we would sleep in the same bed and cuddle, I really liked that. In the bed, he liked to wrestle me even if it meant he would lose. Once when he held me in a head lock, I placed my head there, I allowed him to play in my hair and I could see in his eyes how much he wanted what I physically had as a female. That's when my nephew became curious as to our other physical differences, but at the time I didn't know how to really make him understand, so we didn't explore that subject.

…then I began to grow hair between my legs. I liked the way my "fuzz" felt as I ran my fingers over it. I spent hours, or at least that's the way it seemed back then, cleaning the area. I gently rubbed the soap in a light circular motion in order to clean it. Then I would get a cup of warm water and stand over the toilet and pour it over my area. I had to make certain that I straddled the toilet. I didn't realize how warm the water felt. Then I would pat dry my area with a fluffy towel. But the patting felt so nice, that I would forget how long I was patting my area.

You know I used to add just a little hair grease to it, my area, hoping for the day when I could braid the strands. I eventually got my hairs to the point where I could brush it and it lay in a wavy form, it looked like waves from the ocean! I wanted to keep the wavy form in tact so I would pat folded pieces of toilet paper over it so that my panties would not disrupt the form.

I was becoming comfortable with this new change when my development took a turn for the worse when I started to grow some breasts. Why do these things happen all at once? Is it so my body can get over the change as quickly as possible and get back to normal? They felt like knots and were stiff. I had trouble at first lying in bed on my stomach, geez they hurt. But I liked how they protruded through my shirts. I became so aware of them that I, instead of being proud that I had the signs of becoming a woman, that I sulked to prevent the looks I was now getting from my family. My mother was so proud of the slow and steady signs of my evolution and she gave me space to explore this change in my body. My sisters sometimes comforted me but on other occasions, lied about what was going to happen and conjured stories of what never happened to them as they went through the change. The stories sometimes scared me. In believing what they told me once, I had actually used an elastic "ace" bandage and wrapped my breasts in it. I was so tight that it was hard to breathe. Besides it itched so bad that I was eventually caught rubbing that area profusely. It wasn't until my shortening of breath and the constant reddening that showed in my face that my mother inquired about what was wrong. She laughed a bit and explained that no matter what I did, there was no way to keep them from growing unless I had them removed, permanently! Oh, if I would've seen just one of my sisters that day! Because of that act, I had to wear a cold compress to alleviate the pain and wear some very loose fitting shirts during the healing process. I had no trouble with that part.

On another occasion, my sisters convinced me, even after the breast incident that I should try to prevent my urine from getting into my precious by putting a small piece of cloth in there. Well they didn't explain to me how to do it, nor did they inform me that the dryness would hurt and the last, that I had the most difficult time removing it! I can remember how I had to clinch my teeth in pain and at the same time prevent my mother from noticing when she stood at my bedroom door asking me if I was okay. It took another trip to the bathroom before I got the wad removed with just soaking in the tub.

Those days were rough but as I reflect, I truly believed that my childhood was typical. It wasn't until my sisters were dating that my world would change. I never stopped admiring my sisters and how much freedom they were given to explore and enjoy their moments. They often took me where they went, but as they dated, they spent less time taking me places and talking with me.

I recall a moment when my oldest sister had a guy come over and we all had to pretend that our family was the best. The guy was nervous and my father whispered something in his ear before he sat down. The guy's eyes sort of widened and he tried to clear his throat. I noticed that my father waited until the guy became comfortable before he would occasionally stare at him. That didn't last long this particular night because my father had to leave that night to go back to work because of some big project. He didn't want to go and waited until the last minute; actually he left out and waited until my sister thought he had left for work. My oldest sister was a bit surprised when our father was back at the door ringing the door bell for my sister to answer it. Boy did she look stunned. But after all the activity, my younger sister and I were instructed to go upstairs and not to come back down by our mother.

All of this pretending just piqued my curiosity to no end. So I tried taking a peek downstairs to see what the two of them were doing. I couldn't imagine how my mother didn't hear the noises my sister and the guy were making. As I sat on a step just above the clearing of the ceiling, I positioned myself close to the wall, under the shadows. From this vantage point I could see the guy with hands under my sister's shirt and her dancing some sort of dance. Her eyes sorta rolled, her arms moved with a flailing and as if they had a mind of their own. It was as if her arms could not decide whether or not to grab the guy or franticly twitch in the air with affirmation. Whatever. Anyway, that's when I noticed how much my sister enjoyed what he was doing to her. Her mouth opened and closed as if she was trying to eat a piece of succulent fruit. Her gasps were not loud but on occasion, she sort of drooled a bit and looked down toward him as if silently they both knew what she wanted next.

I was becoming excited, so much that I found myself tugging lightly at my own clothes. I could feel the passion between my sister and her beau and somehow I wanted to be a part of the ongoing feast. But I couldn't move because I would give away my present position. Yet I couldn't look away, because their interaction made me so excited. I wanted to cover my eyes but I didn't want to. Disappointedly, I waited and watched until slowly I fell asleep and my other sister woke me at the same time alerting my older sister of my snooping.

Well in having the upper hand on the devious scheme of my sisters, I realized that my oldest sister figured on the times and days that our father would have to work late. To help in the conspiracy, my younger sister would occupy our mother while my oldest was downstairs enjoying a night of bliss. They had been doing this for some time until I alerted them of my knowing and this was something I treasured. I gained more information from them in parts or in descriptive little notes which they would hold up in my face to read before destroying. This was their way of satisfying me with no accusations because they knew I would tell on them. Knowing what I learned gave me my own permission to seek out a similar suitor for my own experimentation. But that had to wait.

My opportunity first came in the mistake of my sisters. Their planning of figuring out our father's weekly schedule came to a halt in the form of befriending a fellow female classmate whose mother knew of the late scheduling our father had as well as working in the same department with him. Well, one of my sisters started to attract a suitor who was also interested in this female classmate and the tables turned. My sisters' plans were busted right before their eyes and they were punished for allowing me to escape from my room to view. For days my sisters suffered backbreaking chores and the embarrassing presence of our parents showing up at their school at all odd times.

So instead of learning from this ordeal, my sisters came up with a scheme to indulge themselves until such time that they could visit their boyfriends again. In order to accomplish this task, one of my sisters watched me while the other pursued her moment of pleasure. Sometimes the moment took forever! I know this because I couldn't use the bathroom upstairs to have my own private moment of release. I hated looking through my mother's magazines of furniture and kitchen things while I sat bored waiting for one of my sisters to finish.

But once again my careless sisters allowed me the chance

to roam about the house and to look through things. This is where I found their toy. It seemed huge and was a chocolate color. As I handled it in my hand, it was a bit flimsy and I couldn't squeeze it tightly. Another thing that caught my attention about this toy was that it was missing the other male parts that hung below. The toy even had a spot where there should be a hole, interesting. So, when I got the chance to ask my younger sister about the toy, she covered my mouth in the hallway upstairs and looked about before dragging me into her room to question me.

Here she grabbed my arms tightly and asked me how and where did I get the toy. I explained that it was in her boot in the back of her closet. Before I could finish, my eldest sister came in and again, with a finger in my face, questioned me until I became confused as to who to answer first. That's when my eldest sister calmed down, whispered to my other sister and then they both calmed down. I didn't know what they were talking about but I knew it involved me. They started to explain what the toy was used for and I asked them whom the toy resembles since they explained that this was a man's appendage. I already knew that! They went on and on until what they were explaining became boring. What did catch my attention was when they said this toy was too big for me. At first I didn't know what they meant by this toy being too big for me but I asked and when they explained, just thinking about it hurt, oh my.

This only piqued my curiosity more and on another occasion, I gave this toy a try. I found out quickly how no matter what I tried to use to smooth out the insertion of this toy, it would never fit and it started to hurt. Now, I'm not sure why I tried to do this but as I recalled, my sisters had some practice with this curiosity. I wanted to see for myself how they were able to enjoy this toy. So again, I waited and this wait took another week or so before I was being watched by my second sister while my oldest enjoyed her moment. I finally got upstairs without the knowledge of my younger sister and opened the door to my oldest sister's room. There I could see her in action with her toy. What was even more interesting was that she only had on a t-shirt and some sweat

socks. She kicked and shook and leaned back all the while
shoving this thing back and forth until...until... She turned over
and look at me with wild in her eyes. In her astonishment, she
rolled over on her side and covered herself with a towel and one of
the bed sheets. My oldest sister was looking at me with a moist
face and perched lips, but I could tell she was somewhere else on
another planet. My younger sister hadn't heard a sound from us
and I waited for her movements from downstairs, but nothing. My
oldest put her finger to her lips to tell me to be quiet and motioned
for me to close the door. I obliged and then see called for me to
come over to sit near her on the bed. She made me promise not to
tell and if I didn't she would buy me a toy like the one she owned.
She explained to me that she was "playing". I wanted something
else but she insisted that this was the substitute for her boyfriend
until they would meet again. She went to say that until I had a
boyfriend it would be best that I try to use this type of toy. She
offered her advice that she would teach me to play with this toy. I
pondered this for a moment and asked could I have my very own,
one that my sisters wouldn't be able to use. She agreed and then
she sent me downstairs and I forgot about my sneaking past my
younger sister, who as she approached me noticed our sister at the
top of the stairs that indicated this time I was okay.

I behaved myself for a long time, days, weeks even. I
didn't spy on either of my sisters as they continued to take turns
enjoying their moment. However, my patience was wearing thin
and I tried to hold on until I just couldn't anymore. My younger
sister was upstairs enjoying her turn one night and I tiptoed
upstairs until I arrived at her room. Here I waited and waited until
I heard sounds and then I made my move. I opened the door
quietly, knelt down on the floor and waited for my sister to
acknowledge me. She didn't, I moved across the floor until I
reached the side of the bed and waited some more. I could hear the
low moan from my sister and that's when I jumped up to surprise
her. Well this time was my most alarming. What and how my
sister was able to maneuver with her toy was something I would
later come to understand. But she remained stuck in this twisted

position as I surprised her and she wanted to know if I could give her a hand. I said no, ran to the door, closed it lightly and hurried down the stairs where my older sister met me and explained that the toy deal was off. This hurt and I blamed my younger sister for hurting my chance. All I ever wanted was to be like the two of them.

My cursing of my sisters' very existence paid off with their home experiences spilling into rumors at their school which prompted our parents to revisit their initial punishment for them. On a particular night I got to witness just how much of a punishment our parents could inflict if disobeyed. My mother made my sisters first take off all their clothes down to their underwear (hah, the panties that my sisters were wearing were funny; cartoons, with ruffles at the legs and waist, hah) run up and down the stairs and as each came to the main floor, our mother, waiting, would smack them each with a thin belt across whatever she could hit, except for their faces. Our mother ran them silly until they couldn't walk up or down the steps. The sad part was when my younger sister, crying, screaming and begging our mother to stop actually stopped midway on the steps. Well mother moved past my older sister, hitting her on the way up and began swinging in all directions at my younger sister. All that she could do was holding up her arms to absorb the hits and then she tried to hold up one of her legs for extra protection. Unfortunately, by doing all of this, she caused herself to tumble down the few steps to the main floor. This didn't stop mother who turned with the belt held high in the air, but first hitting my older sister again as she passed, and followed my sister down the steps until she came to a stop. At the same time, my older sister, whimpering, stopped on the steps near the upstairs landing and our mother then had to choose to ascend the steps to attend to her or stay on the main floor and finish up on my younger sister. The whacking stopped and our mother yelled epithets at both of them before ascending the stairs past my older sister and entered her room, slamming the door behind her.

Later what I discovered after listening in on my parents was that it was one of my sisters apparently borrowed one of the toys that belonged to our parents. It was missing, or at least that how it sounded from my room. Later, our father began gathering things into a box from my parents' room and packing them into his car. He kept walking back and forth past the three of us as we sat in the living room, carrying a box to the car and then bringing back a different box. My sisters began quietly chattering amongst themselves in a low whisper each time our parents left our presence. Soon after we heard our father drive off with the boxes and return later that night with two identical suitcases, one light green and the other light blue. Our mother met him in the living room where he placed the two suitcases near the steps and the two of them went into the kitchen, turn on some music and began whispering. We could faintly hear the two of them talking back and forth for awhile then silent and then back to talking. They spoke in a rampant pace each time and then the conversation would tail off. When they came out, the two of them walked to the stairs silently and took both suitcases upstairs, eventually summoning my sisters upstairs. I was told not to come upstairs. So, I listened quietly for more punishment, but all I kept hearing was crying and pleading from my sisters.

This was the beginning to my sisters being sent to a summer camp for girls only and my being sent away to my grandparents' home for the entire summer. I would later find out that this staying over my grandparents would last a bit longer than expected. However, my parents explained it this way to me; that I had to stay with my grandparents until they could find another school for me. This was because the school I was currently attending could no longer guarantee the separation of both mainstream students on the main wing of the school and students who required special attention, like me. Also the school didn't have an afterschool program for students with special attention needs and the bus service did not run long after school hours. As I listened I would find out that my sisters and I were attending similar schools except their school was the higher grade school and on another side of the school campus. In addition, I would be at home alone during the summer while my sisters were away. This was something my parents didn't want for me. I didn't know that I needed someone to look after me all the time. I just thought we (the family) liked spending time with one another when I came home from school. These decisions came sudden and I wasn't able to understand why this was happening. Again the real reason was something I would later find out. The now part was something I wasn't expecting and I would miss being with my friends. However this gave me another opportunity to explore my new found knowledge that my sisters had given me. I hadn't given that any thought until now.

I never gave it any thought, you know, what we were doing. We were only practicing what I had seen before. All I wanted to do was experiment. Actually I did kinda like it, well, I really like it. I thought my nephew would like that, the experiment. Besides, it wasn't going to hurt either of us. After all I had seen, heard and was shown, who wouldn't want to try what I did? Besides I'm not for certain but I could tell he had always wanted to try it...even with me but was just afraid of asking me. This was his chance to try it before he got into trouble with any other girl. He was told the same thing that was told to me. We had the same reasons to try it, together. You know, I could help him, with that, the learning and he could help keep me satisfied.

I didn't realize that from the time we started how much we had grown. I hadn't seen him in a while and he was still trusting of me. At this point I had grown tired of experimenting on myself because it took too much time and it had become boring. I had tried other positions with other types of toys from around the house but to do so meant that I had to apply more effort. So here we are, he was curious and I had some experience, he always wanted to try and I needed to try a different version.

I never thought that he was so curious to sneak a peek at me. He could've just asked me. But I did like the way he looked at me just before we got started. Oh the amazement in his eyes! It was so beautiful to see such innocence and interest all at the same time. But my nephew seemed reluctant as if I was going to tell even in the midst of our endeavor. It was hard to assure him and he wanted to back out at the last minute. I couldn't let him do that to us. After I had made the arrangements and set up everything for him to get his wish and he tried to blow it for the both of us. It was easy once we got started and he was very thankful that we did. He looked so relieved when he left. After our first encounter, he seemed more interested in playing, I like playing. So since he wanted to and I wanted to, we just kept helping each other to play.

Then there was my other nephew. He seemed scared of almost everything. He was smaller than my favorite nephew but he looked up to him, so I assumed he would look up to me. The whole thing we encountered was more of a mistake, you see, my favorite wasn't visiting that weekend. For whatever reason, that bitch of a mother of his wouldn't let him come over for a visit. I always hated her.

Anyway, that weekend after I had taken a bath, I think that's what I did, I left the bathroom a little damp. There wasn't anyone upstairs at the time and I could hear my other nieces and nephews out on the porch. So I had planned to return to the bathroom to drain and clean the tub, but as I removed my towel to dry off, a breeze hit me. It felt so cool on this summer day and I tried to bask in the moment. As I did, a sensation came over me. It felt so relaxing, refreshing and so cool. I wanted to enjoy it more so I laid on my bed on my back with my legs bent at my knees and closed my eyes. I don't how long I stayed there but I heard a noise downstairs. I opened my eyes to search about for the source of the noise and could only hear some movement downstairs. It sounded like it was coming from the kitchen. So I waited and waited until I could hear movement coming out of the kitchen. I got out of my bed, wrapped my towel around me and stood near my doorway. I heard the noise pause and then I could hear quick movements. I yelled in the direction of the movement, "…hey?" I could hear a pause and a slow quiet response. I yelled to whoever it was to come upstairs. There was another long pause and started to become irritated and impatient. So I yelled threats and eventually I could hear movement ascending the stairs.

There he stood scared with chocolate on his left hand where he forgot to like it off. I explained it was a good thing our grands weren't downstairs to catch him. I knew where they had gone but he didn't. He had those pleading eyes and I knew then that he would do anything to stay out of trouble, plus I wasn't finished with my wind bath. So I asked him would he help me. He said yes and I reached out so that he could grab my hand. When he did, I turned and lightly pulled him to me.

Like my favorite nephew, my nephew did what I asked without hesitation. He didn't seem nervous and I asked if he wanted to do this again later. I'm not sure if he said yes, but let's just say he did, because he didn't want to get in trouble or disappoint me. So we continued our visits until my favorite came back to bring me the relief I needed. Until then my other nephew was the holding place.

Humiliation

My cousin wanted the birthday party at his house for my eldest daughter. He said that he is never asked to host any family gatherings. I didn't have the heart to tell him that often the company he kept had a lot to do with that. No one could keep up with the many female friends he kept. Oftentimes he would have one in the morning and another that evening. I didn't care but in his company it sometimes became confusing and I tried to never remember their names. But he was different about this occasion and persistent about this gathering. My cousin wanted to show off his current girlfriend and their commitment to staying together for over a year and a half. My wife was enthusiastic about this arrangement because she had developed a good relationship with my cousin's current girlfriend. This one was different in my opinion. She really had a way of bringing out the best in my cousin's demeanor and that moved my wife. She kept the girlfriend close to her side and she introduced her to everyone as a permanent fixture.

Many family members tried to stay to meet up with others whom they hadn't seen in a while. It just seemed impossible to have all the family members who were visiting together at once because of prior commitments or that they just didn't want to stay. Of course our niece's parents came and they and my wife discussed many issues surrounding my niece. Even my "grands" made the visit and congratulated my eldest with money. They moved about with less effort, I could tell that even at their age that a moment like this was not going to be hampered by time and that they would make every effort to stay as long as they could stand the commotion.

All was going well and I finally had the chance to sit and to talk with my cousin. With all that was going on lately, we missed opportunities to have our usual discussions about us, life and the sort. When I had decided to wait for the right time to catch my cousin alone, I saw him heading for the house. Not to be anxious about having the opportunity to speak with him, I waited a little longer. Eventually I entered the house and listened for any sounds. Nothing. So I decided to move through the living room into the dining room off to the side. From there I could hear someone turn on the faucet. So, I entered the kitchen and found him sitting taking in the moment of the family gathering. By the time I sat with him, we probably had a good "buzz" from our drinking. He had a glass of wine in front of him and I could see the other unopened bottles on the counter. Eventually I sat down and we began a slow conversation. We sat laughing and joking about the night with my neighbor and all the other trouble we had experienced. My cousin kept steering the conversation to the moment between the girl and I. He kept the pressure on me to tell him what was said that night. I believe he thought I either lied about what occurred or left things out. We went back and forth for a time until I broke.

I began to tell him, but before I started I paused. in preparation, my cousin gathered his faculties and erased the smile from his face. He waited and I didn't disappoint him. I tried to lead us back to our aunt and some of the things she had done to us when we were younger. This was a tricky task because my cousin often swayed back and forth emotionally with this subject. I could never tell when the right time to talk to him about this was. Right now it seemed like a good time to find healing and closure emotionally, if just a little. We had been drinking and he was a little more receptive for the moment. We rarely talked long enough to come to any conclusion to our dilemma, but I always tried when the time permitted. I was trying to find a way, but I wasn't going to tell him my troubles coping with that period in our lives. He often joked like the entire fiasco was a rite of passage for us. But today I was looking for a positive and sincere response from him.

It wouldn't have to come to this point, but we had heard that our aunt was to have come to this party. When I was informed I immediately looked over the crowd for my cousin who hadn't yet heard the news. I had to wait some time later to see this same informant of a relative talk to my cousin with the same information. After he heard the news, it didn't take long for my cousin to visually search for me amongst family. When he found me, our eyes just locked for a while and that was the indication of our revelation. We made arrangements to meet as soon as possible to find out what the other heard or knew from the informant relative.

So this uneasiness moved me to drink a little more this day to subdue my fear and concern. I had not seen my aunt in years! It had been well over ten years. I pondered this for a moment to picture how she changed in physical appearance and how much would have changed in her mannerism. But I could not formulate a picture in my mind beyond the thought. My cousin was another subject. I wasn't sure how long between the last times that my cousin had seen her.

So here we were, we sat playing with the subject. My cousin talked to me in a tone that indicated his stubbornness to concede to discussing the subject. He slowly stood up and pushed the chair under the table. I surmised that we were not going to find a place to start and if we did, we weren't going to stay there very long. But I had finally found a focal point; his girlfriend. I started in with the fact that one day he might have a flashback or she would do something to him that would bring about a past reaction. My cousin became offended with the suggestion and direction of the conversation and angrily explained that he wouldn't mentioned this to his girlfriend. I pressed him with how was their relationship going thus far. He explained that she was the most understanding and giving person he had met in some time. I inquired about how he met her. My cousin paused and asked me what the importance of the question was. I tried to explain, but at that point he cut me off and said he met her at the library. I was taken, my cousin in a library, wow. He waited for me to throw a joke at him about it, but I didn't. Instead I asked about his visit to the library. He said it was nothing. I again pressed him more until he said that he was looking up some terms and some books on things. I realized that maybe he was looking into what was going on inside his own head or maybe what could be done about what he felt about what our aunt did to him. My cousin wouldn't budge any more than what I had already pushed on him. Instead he changed the subject back to me and my wife. I wasn't expecting that and he went further into painting a picture of my telling my wife about my past that I've kept from her. He also explained that I should think about doing the same for my wife's sake. We stayed focused on his not telling his girlfriend when he reminded me of the girl at the club.

I had forgotten about that for a moment because the focus was not on me but rather on him. He sat back down looking at me trying to impress upon me the look and attention of an eight year old. It bothered me to tell him about what was actually discussed that night, but I needed to bond with him because of our aunt's possible visit. So I told him the story of what really happened that night at the club and he sat there motionless. He had never heard the term "let's play". He was surprised that our aunt even had names for what we were doing. He explained that he was given the term, "come and let's comfort each other" by our aunt when we were younger. I sat back possibly with the same reaction he had just given by me. We sat there analyzing the terms we were given that neither one of us knew the other was given.

My cousin continued with his questions by asking how did it make me feel, the "let's play" question. I tried to assure him that in all the times I've heard it from friends, relatives or even coworkers, when that girl asked that question that night, in my own mind everything around me went dark. I said to him that I could see our aunt asking me that same question, starting on her escapade.

Again, we both sat there dumbfounded, unable to find the words to continue our conversation, wrapped up in reminiscing over the many encounters we had individually and the few we had together with our aunt. I had never heard my cousin ask me the next set of questions, but they came in sequence. He first asked me was I ever scared when I first had my experience with our aunt. I explained yes and he explained he was terrified and wanted to look for me. When he did find me he was angry because I did not come to his rescue nor did I try to seek help once I found out. That was comforting to both of us, because I explained that was one of the reasons we would get into fights when our aunt was around the both of us. His next question seemed a bit offensive but I answered as truthfully as I could. My cousin asked me if I ever enjoyed the moments with our aunt. I again explained that it felt good as I got older but every experience made me feel more emotionally displaced. I went on to say that I was afraid of her for some time up until I was about fourteen and I saw just how bigger I was when I was over her. I continued with at times what I did with my aunt helped to give me some relief because I was suppressing my urges at that age. My cousin wondered how I was trapped in that scene long after it stopped with him. I gave a look of surprise. My thoughts were our aunt had continued with him just as long as she did with me! My cousin shot back and explained that he thought since he was eldest between us that our aunt would end the encounters with him. I asked him to recall when was his last time with her. He started in a low voice, hesitant, and then he said the last time was almost a year earlier than my last encounter! We were both in our early teens and my last encounter was sometime around my birthday. That would mean that our aunt did the same to my cousin because he is almost year older than me. I asked him how he knew about what our aunt was doing to me and he explained that there was always a look and mannerism in me after my encounter. I added to his statement by saying that I too knew when he had some of his encounters with our aunt.

We sat back quietly and with thoughts far beyond where we sat at that moment. As our moment of silence rolled on, my cousin finally asked me how the last time ended with our aunt. I explained that it ended with our aunt trying to take off my pants and getting them down to my knees. She then stuck her hand into my boxers and proceeded to message me when I thought of my girlfriend at that time. With that thought I began to ask her to stop. She asked what was wrong and I said to her that I'd rather take off my own clothes. She obliged and swiftly took off her clothes and started for the bed when I turned to leave. My aunt grabbed me by the arm and began badgering me with threats of abuse, rape and some other things I just couldn't remember. I explained that there was nothing anyone would believe in this situation because she was to be the adult and I was still a kid. My cousin's eyes began to well. I didn't stop at that point; I needed to go on for the both of us. I went on to say that our aunt started to beg me, plead with me and even wanted to pay me for the act. I could see the first tear pushing its way out from my cousin's eye. I had to move on. Continuing, I told him that she started to climb all over me explaining that I had truly satisfied her and there could be no other. At this point I wanted to stop, but now the tears kept flowing out of my cousin's eyes. I said I turned towards our aunt's direction, looked at her straightway and hard, and explained that if this was true, then why did she start on my cousin, her other nephew. My cousin had wiped away his tears and started to blow his now running nose. I felt light-headed and moved to get another drink when my cousin just went into his own spill of events.

My cousin started with the first time when I was away at my new house and he and his sisters came over to visit our grands. He continued with while there at our grands on a particular night, it was thundering and lightning a great deal. He was awakened by the booming, crackling and bright light of the storm and had become scared. He looked over for his sisters who were now sharing the same room and they were already gone to another room closer to our grands. That's when he heard a low voice asking him was he okay. He says he called out to see who was asking him that question, for a moment he thought of goblins and the sort. Just when he started to panic, he noticed that the voice was from our aunt. She explained to him that his sisters were in the room next to our grands and she wanted to know if he was alright in the room by himself. He explained that he was trying to be tough but he finally admitted he was a bit concerned about being alone. So our aunt climbed into bed with him and before he knew it she had pretended to be scared also and asked him to come and let's comfort each other. My cousin pushes away from the table and turns his back to me as he heads to the sink. With his head bowed, he starts in a voice that increases in decibels that he honestly thought that night that he was helping her. My cousin looks about the kitchen with a disgusted expression, his hands clinching as if he's trying to crush something with each hand. He turns in another direction, turns back to me and explains in not so much detail how that night our aunt made him do so many things that he had become raw for a while. He went on to say that the next morning when he came downstairs our aunt acted as if nothing ever happened to the contrary. My cousin tries to laugh about it but explains that this moment occurred in that summer before I had to spend that summer with him when I had gotten in trouble at my new home. I took another gulp of the wine and played with the glass, spinning it lightly.

I slouched in my kitchen chair while my cousin eased back into the chair opposite me with another filled glass and asked me, "What are we going to do about what we just said"? I wasn't ready to answer that so I asked my cousin how he was holding up with his experiences with other females since he had stopped being involved with our aunt. He looked over at me and explained that for a long time he had trouble with relationships sexually and sometimes emotionally. My cousin tried to give examples of his misguided attempt to truthfully try to experience a sexual act with a girl only to fall into some Jekyll and Hyde type person with uncontrolled anger and intent. He went on to say some girls were scared to the point they went along but didn't want to interact with him thereafter. Other girls, he says, liked some of that stuff but at times he was too intense as if he couldn't be satisfied. He gulps down all of what was left in his glass, stands up and reaches for another bottle. He comes back to his seat and asks me if I wanted more, I said a little and he pours both of us an evenly portion. My cousin plays with his glass after taking another long gulp and asks me how my relationships went before meeting my wife. I explained that I encountered many of the same type of moments with females but that I was afraid that I might infect one of them with what we have. I didn't want to talk about this part because I knew that my cousin hadn't taken his prison to that level. My cousin leans back with small laughter and asks me what I meant by infection or infecting someone else. I started to elaborate on my position of what has happened to us and how we are beset with this disease which causes a little bit of a different reaction but mainly the same. My cousin denies that he doesn't have this so called disease and that it happened to us because our parents didn't want to see the problem. Continuing he yells out that our aunt, grandparents and any other adult family member should burn in hell for their part in masquerading this entire fiasco. There was nothing I could say. For the first time I realized that for whatever reason, many of our older family members, like our other aunts, uncles, family adult friends and yes, our grandparents and parents had to have known something and just ignored what was going on. I wanted to dig further into how my cousin obtained this revelation, so I asked him what incidents gave him this notion. He couldn't wait to give me one incident after the other. He spoke about the time one of our uncles who were much older than our aunt came up stairs to investigate why we were not outside and everyone else was out. At this point he says that we were in our aunt's room and our aunt was hiding in her closet and all we could say was that we were playing, but our uncle explained to us to not mess with anything in the room and to leave shortly. Another incident he says was when our aunt use to call us up stairs individually to help her with something and our grands would on occasion inquire why we were going upstairs. My cousin leaned forward to look for a sign in any of my gestures to see my revelation. I was a bit dumbfounded that I hadn't come up with an answer. He said we were told by our aunt to say we were going to go upstairs to do a number two, a NUMBER TWO! He tells me to think hard on these two incidents and tell him why we were not questioned more and then given the alternative. He continued to say we should've been sent out of our aunt's room because first, she's a female and he poses the question, "What's in a female's room that a male would need to see, use or even play with?" He had me there but I had to come to terms of how people knew what was happening to us or at the very least some idea that something was not right and then to build in their mind a disbelief of the circumstances. I asked my cousin did he know of anyone in particular that he believes knew what was going on with us all the time. I was asking because a little panic was setting in and I was hoping that there wasn't anyone for my own relief. He sat back for a moment and thought hard about this, playing with his glass. I was hoping all the while that he couldn't come up with a single name and that would be the end of someone else knowing about our moments. It would've been hard to fathom someone else knowing of this act and not doing anything about it, even to this day. This would throw me over the edge because then I knew we were not alone and that there was help out there that never came to our rescue. I gave into a wild thought that whoever knew was allowing it to happen because it happened to them or that they didn't know what to do in that matter. Any decision would've been better than leaving us there to be subjected to such an affliction that still bothers us up to this day. My cousin seemed numb to the thought, his mind was already made up in confronting who knew. I could see the anger and revenge in his eyes. He was fixated with a focused determination. All he had to do was find out who knew and he would just walk right up to them and expose everything, it didn't matter to him who heard it. But I decided to venture further to know more as an outsider as well as an insider what my cousin was going through in dealing with this disease.

I started into our next part of the subject with asking him why he continued after he was old enough to know the difference. My cousin explained that he was so use to it and became so bottled up with emotion as to what to do or say that by the time the moment was over he was just glad it stopped. I asked him as he got older did he release inside her. He looked at me with a hard stare, clinched his teeth at me and faked at me with a lunge that made me flinch a little. I could see that he was fighting the tears and then it hit me that at that at our ages, we could've gotten our aunt pregnant. I couldn't begin to think what that would do for either of us once we were found out. Then another thought sank in deeper because we hadn't seen our aunt in such a long time that maybe that was one of the reasons she just disappeared for awhile. I moved my hand slowly over my mouth in a gasp, looked over to my cousin who was sinking fast into his seat and was allowing the pain to surface. I reached over to him to apologize and to empathize. He held my hand in a handshake, looked up at me with a slow running nose and a well of fluid in his eyes. I found myself with the same symptoms but I was trying to verbalize and found that my mouth was full of saliva as I began to cough because of the filling in my mouth. All I could do was swallow and I pulled my hand away from my cousin to hold my face. It seems as if my cousin was in the distance as he began to cry with convulsions until he tried to stand to stop the flow of emotion. I gathered myself and stood, walking in another direction, wiping the tears on my sleeve and trying to choke back what was left. My cousin finally stood and turned to again stand over the sink. He turned on the water at a high pressure and began to draw the accumulation of salvia in his mouth into a blob to release it into the sink. He spit and I could hear the blob hit the galvanized bowl with a loud spat. He didn't move at first, I guess he was using this moment as a catalyst for the next. He kept staring into the sink and I kept staring in his direction.

We had not realize how long we sat dealing with our demons and attempting to find some closure with the guilt and blame we burdened ourselves with all these years. I realize that is why we stayed so close because we knew that each of us was an individual victim as well as collective one, besides, we were the brother neither of us had. My cousin was gaining his composure and uses the running water to splash and wipe across his face until it dripped from his nose and chin. I grabbed several paper towels and shoved them into his hands before nudging him to the side of the sink to take my turn. He looked up and pushed back lightly not allowing me full access. I looked over at him and he gave me a look of innocence as well as a look of concern about the problem I was having in getting to the sink.

To our happiness, satisfaction or relief, our aunt never showed up and as the day was turning into nightfall, many family members started to discuss missing other members. This was when we found out some of the issues that plagued our aunt and why she was sent to our grands for the summer. But her stay lasted longer than just a mere visit for the summer. It turned out to be the initial summer, then back home for a few months, then back again and then she just stayed. But when her stay was extended, her parents started to come by less and less. About this same time no one had seen her sisters.

Our aunt's affliction, disease or whatever you want to call it was never an issue because it was understood by other family members that our aunt's parents and her sisters always had problems. My aunt's family had problems that were the kind which called for medical attention, and even worse, permanent placement. This was one of the reasons why my aunt's sisters were not seen for quite some time nor would her family visit as often as everyone would like. We tried to dig a little deeper but the conversation started to tail off and we knew that another moment like this would not surface for quite some time. My cousin showed no emotion regarding what he had heard but I digested this information, even the little we obtained. I wanted to develop a plan of attack where I could inquire more about my aunt from other family members. The question I toyed with was how could I approach them without giving away my intent? This I would continue to ponder.

Eventually my wife came over to tell me it was time to leave and that we needed to bid farewell to our niece's parents. Reluctantly I moved wife's direction, passing my cousin and his girlfriend. My cousin and quickly discussed our next step and that we would be in contact with each other later. As I approached my niece's parents I could see the trust and happiness that they bestowed upon us for our generosity for keeping their daughter. My cousin-in-law grabbed my hand and hugged me in a brotherly fashion, almost lifting me up. At that moment I could see my niece looking on for a moment and our eyes locked before she walked off to catch up with my youngest daughter.

Amalgamation

The day has been a little dreary and somehow this weather pattern has moved over to infect everyone's attitude in the house with a lull. However, to prevent giving into this feeling, the kids have somehow come together to go as a group to the movies for a double header. The "wifey" found a partner in crime (her girlfriend from down the street) to join her in a day on the town and she was off not too long after the kids had left the house. That left me again, to entertain my prison. So off I went to prepare, but first I had to get comfortable. The mood had to be set just right. I just couldn't jump right into this ordeal of enjoying my prison, but instead I had to build it up, slowly with care. But, this is where things start to become weird. I entered my bedroom for a moment and sat in the lounge chair next to the bed. As I removed my shoes, I realize that I haven't had many moments with my cohort lately and now is the ultimate time to venture where no one else can go with me. So I try a little reflection first with my prison on our last adventure. This will allow me to not replicate my last moment with my prison.

But this will not be that day. I've thought about it, roamed around the house playing games of avoidance with my prison only for it to call my name. When it does, there's no response from me. I thought I was going crazy for a moment, but I haven't responded to its call like I had in the past. I can hear my prison, see it in action, but this is where my prison has been held in check. It's strange to see something that has held you for so long as a prisoner or as a captured prey but never eaten, all of a sudden broken. I'm looking at my prison and I can see the bonds it has held me with, no longer there. I ask myself, "...is this real?" I try to think harder upon its call...but again nothing. I'm not disgusted by the situation, just amazed. I keep telling myself that I've conquered my most formidable foe. This is a foe-friend of mine which I have allowed to torment me for so long. I am cured, but I know this will be short lived because I have experienced being in this same situation before and saw myself defeated my prison. But soon again, I was at its beckoning call, a weak dependent to it as I carried out its plan of incompetent pleasure. The unfortunate part of my insistence to enjoy this moment is that I've somehow lost a connection with my prison. I can't place where it is lost and yet I'm looking for a way to revive it in the process. Yet I have not admitted to myself as to why I can't connect to it right now. With reluctance I start to give into the thought which has been the mechanism holding me back from my prison; I've been holding on to my conversation with my cousin and I can't get it out of my mind.

You see, I'm not sure why my perception of life has begun to change since having that meeting with my cousin, but I've been doing a lot more reflection on just how screwed up I may have become since my first encounter with my aunt. The two of us (my cousin and I) have been connected together in some weird way for too long. I know we have more in common than an incident which has tainted us for most of our lives. Ours (my cousin and I) is a bond that should never have been consummated in that way. This bond has given us an insight into what the other thinks, to some degree, given certain circumstances. This is something (the insight) I would rather not have in my possession. But because of this illegitimate bond, I also have developed characteristics unknown to average people.

This is a physical attribute which only those in similar states of mind can recognize and I am now coming to terms with for myself. I have come across people who have demonstrated these same characteristics and yet I can't, won't, approach them with a indication which will tell them that I know. By doing so would be indirectly an admission of guilt and would expose the other person. That would mean that regardless of the outcome, we would be looked upon as having similar traits. For example, you see a smoker smoke, yet you do not understand the depth in which they go to lengths in order to smoke. Only another smoker can understand and recognize that symptom. We can evaluate, analyze, surmise and recommend to a smoke of the cause and effects of smoking, but until you've had a similar episode with anything that provides you with a prison…So if I can see it in them, have I really masked this trait from them and if so, how can I keep it from them? They are not of my kind. This sounds prejudicial, but true like minds understand that not all prisons are alike. The underlying symptom of a prison is there, such as the association to almost everything, the constant searching for stimuli for your prison and of course the moment to enjoy your prison. The prison is like that of driving a car. There are many out there and they all contain for the most very standard components, but you have a choice as to which one you want. This is where we sometimes compare cars as one having greater functionality than the other. I don't think we can go that far in comparing prisons in that way. Some prisons inflict great devastation on the body inside or outside. Other prisons are in the patterns of habit and those can affect other people. These cannot be compared to others that inflict the body. At least this is way I see it. But as I said this before, this is where the similarities end. My prison would shock the shit out of a smoker or addict or alcoholic. To the contrary, some of the ways an addict succumbs to obtaining a fix to their prison might offend me. Or the way a person with obsessive compulsive disorder who deals with habits or perfection. I don't knock people with that type of prison, but comparing that prison to my prison would make a person with O.C.D. feel very safe. Therefore all prisons are looked at with some scrutiny as a whole, nothing more. Besides would you want to be called something that you're not? It would be quite hard to defend that you're not being what you demonstrate as having some particular affliction. So there are limits we holders of the prisons uphold in comparison to one another.

The reason why I say this is because I've recently discovered some alarming emotional characteristics about myself. One such emotional state is that I've realized how "revved-up" I get in anticipation of having an intimate moment with my wife. Now on the other hand I have come to realize how my intense build up of the anticipated encounter also triggers me to become agitated as the moment nears. To add to this state of being, I can also sense how my body temperature is elevated to some degree. Then again this part could be in my own mind, but I do feel a heighten temperature within my body. In addition, I tend to stay "revved-up" longer after a encounter and eventually I intensify the slightest encounter with my wife thereafter. I mean, if you can imagine, in the wild where there are two lions about to mate. The female sends out the signal that the time has come for her to copulate, but she is a bit unsettled by the fact that she now has to go forward with this emotional state. She is not accustomed to this state of being and it causes her to change her daily way of life. In other words, this can be a burdened to her. At least this is how I've seen it. Now take the male lion that has picked up this scent and now knows that the female is ready to copulate. The male too has mixed emotions on having to go forth with this interactive moment. He first has to found out if he's the one she will choose for this endeavor or if he is chosen, then is he the only one chosen? This would mean that he would either have to fight or he is next in line behind the dominant male. This same male lion who has been chosen will have to find the best approach to keeping the female settled while he performs his lion duties in the moment. It is my belief at this point that neither one truly knows how to deal with this intensity. When the two lions are now about to indulge, they show their teeth, growl, fidget, move with alternating twitches even before the moment. Their senses are heightened. However, the two must do this act a couple of times before, by their physical make-ups, there have been enough interaction in the moment to warrant an ending. Now I'm not saying my wife and I have had an encounter similar to these two lions, but, I thinks it's me, we are in a tense moment before, during and even after our intimate moment.

The alternate side to this encounter is that we, my wife and I, somehow practice this emotional rollercoaster even after our encounter as if one of us has not been satisfied or something. I am not one to even think about bragging or boasting, but I believe in my heart that I have done, tried, experimented with every possible position and act that would bring my wife delight and a yearning for more, this I'm hoping. These beforehand encounters we have are not volatile but they seem to have this same defensive approach and reactively charged answers verbally like the two lions. The situations never go far but the friction rises quickly and then subsides like a rollercoaster. I've tried to replay some of our encounters only to come to a conclusion that most of the time it has been me who have caused this explosive encounter. It's as if I like doing this or that there is something within me that I've never addressed that triggers me to react in such a way. To add to this perplexity, the two of us move forward with sarcasm until we find laughter in our moment and all is well again. Now this makes me wonder that we have not been completely satisfied in our intimate indulgence or is it just me (again) and I have supplanted this behavior in my wife? This is the behavior that I've been exploring and I have not drawn a conclusion to this part of me, yet.

I've tried to equate this behavior to my encounters with my aunt and I can see slight similarities between what I had to practice with her and what I yearn to do with my wife. I know the difference between a need and a want and what I need, and want, is to be with my wife in every way possible. However, my practiced habits with my aunt have scared me into a mannerism that I want to keep separate from my wife. I have never entertained any similarities with my wife while with my wife regarding my aunt. But even though I don't, somehow there is still that part of me which was with my aunt that still surfaces unconsciously. This is a state of mind I can see myself breaking away from, with the greatest of effort, but I never knew that this was that connection I was expressing. I feel for a moment as if my wife has been a catalyst for my aunt.

Another state is that on occasion, I have an insatiable appetite when it comes to my wife and my sexual encounters. What I mean is that my drive to not let go of the moment which oftentimes leaves me exhausted. It's as if I'm fighting within myself to hold onto the moment. I recall how my aunt would experiment with me until I was so tired that she would just leave me there to sleep. There were many times that I would be so raw that it would hurt to urinate. Just the slightest touch in my groin area would cause me to jump in pain. To make matters worse was that I somehow had grown accustomed to the physical demands of my encounter with my aunt. I carried this practice on even when I started to like and pursue girls. But my problem was that this type of behavior of mine carried with it such intensity that I was deemed crazy by some females. However, not all of them were scared. Many wanted me in that way. I swore that I was giving them my infection, so I would "toned" down how intense I would give my prison to them. It was like I had that much control; again this is what I believed.

In frustration I stand up ready to slap myself around for thinking something like that. As I stand I realize how I could've ventured into that line of thinking because of how much I've entertained regarding these habits of mine. But I explain to myself of how removed my aunt has been in my life and how, she (my wife) doesn't know this part about me. My wife has been integral in assisting me in my development of moving on and pass my experiences with my aunt. Many of my past experiences I had to disguise as other female relationships in order to receive my wife's insight on what I could've done differently while I was in them. Oftentimes she would tell me how sorry she felt for me as I portrayed myself as wayward and indecisive in my approach to those phantom relationships. During my charade telling to my wife, she spoke of how she could see the pain I experienced from my past relationships. She went on with telling me that oftentimes those things relative to older experiences such as clothes, scenery and expressions can often hold the link between me and my previous relationships. My wife has also helped me looked into how much of those past experiences that I held on to for no other reason than as a form of not being able to forgive myself. Up to this day my wife hasn't had a reason to know that all of the girls I spoke to her about were my aunt and for now I plan on keeping it that way.

I was warned that this would be the dilemma I would be up against. My cousin explained to me on that day as well as others that he was dealing with this same dilemma with his latest friend and that she has been very supportive to him. But just discussing our past made him not want to continue the conversation with me on that day our aunt (thankfully) was suppose to visit.

Since my cousin and I shared more than what we've shared in a long time, the effects and reactions we've had to our now prisons Is something we are dealing with on an individual basis. I've had moments of reflections since that day my cousin and I talked which had caused me to address myself. Allow me to explain, the interaction with my wife and I, I've been looking at long and recalling many moments, great small, unnecessary, in order to see the effects of my prison. But because of this discussion with my cousin, I've questioned how my hiding of my prison has also affected my wife. I've tried to study how my yearning could turn my wife away or persuade her to play games with me in order to build more on my anticipation. There have been times where she has displayed a look or concern or deep thoughts while we have started to build on our moment together. Again, I'm not for certain and I try to convince myself that I am approaching my condition with some unbiased understanding. But as I can draw no conclusion or definitive fact about my behavior or influence with my wife, I lure myself into reaching beyond her into the realm of the worst of possibilities. By doing this I think I will uncover me in my interactions with others and then I can see if I display those same characteristics with my wife. Thinking about this it makes logical sense to me to continue my venturing.

But as I venture further and further into remembering moments with neighbors, coworkers, people I've met on the street that I may never see again, I can see myself venturing where I don't want to go; my kids. At the instant of my realization, I stop myself in sort of a mild shock. My mouth slowing gapes open to allow the sigh of breath to ease out. I can feel my heart speed up and I began to nervously shake in a light manner. The sweat starts to form instantly along my brow, along my forearms and in my underwear. I try not to entertain this aspect of myself as I have an outer body experience to which I reply to myself with disgust, shame, even hatred. I immediately question myself as to analyze what have I done to my own kids, when, where, for how long, how many times. I can't beat the guilt out of my mind as I race across the weeks, the months, and years of their growing up where I stepped in with my prison and held out my hand for them to take it from me. I can see the moment happening over and over again, my holding out my hand for any one of my kids to grab. Sometimes they fight over who will get to enjoy the prison this time. In another moment none of them want it and two of them decide to push the other into the prison I hold. Another scenario is that I've gathered them altogether to enjoy my prison all at once. I, I sit in my chair in my bedroom unable to shake away my conviction and continue with, looking at how innocent they would be, trusting of me, taking whatever I gave, hoping, knowing that what they are about to receive is good for them. While I sit, I can feel the tears building in my eyes. A tingling of humiliation beats my entire body. I don't know how to console myself with hands. Instead I just let them hang as I lay my forearms across my thighs. Right now I really don't know what to do. I've place myself in a position of motionlessness. As I try to fight the feeling, it hurts, my body aches with every attempt to move. As I continue to break free, all I can see, it's fuzzy, is the same shock I experienced in my kids. The pain holds me a little longer. It's so intense that it feels like a stinging across most of my body. I can only equate it to sitting too long on a toilet before your legs go completely numb. But this stinging hurts like a pain you can't find relief. My mouth opens to cry out and saliva, which has built up in my mouth, flows out uncontrollably. The sound is to low, I thought it came out, that I don't hear it. The saliva extends into a long line until most of it pulls free from what is still connected to my mouth. Some of the droplets land on my now clinched fists that I hold across my body. Even the repulsiveness of the saliva with its bubbles intact can't pull me away from the state of mind I hold. In light of that I start to lean over in a slump questioning myself. All the while I'm still trying to listen for the sounds in my moans of shame. By hearing the sounds this would justify the pain I'm feeling that I physically see on myself. I don't know why I need to see evidence, but I feel I need to also see myself in pain. Maybe by doing this the pain might subside. This moment of back and forth in my mind keeps me occupied. I can't recall how long my state of disrepute lasts but

I know that I don't want to experience it again. I know now that I have led myself to entertain how far my reach can go by holding on to an infection which could kill my children's innocence. I fight with myself to erase this thought of my own doing and even wonder for a split second, am I going crazy over this? But nothing registers within me to alert me of falling over the edge of sanity, yet.

I try to think of ways in which to punish myself for exploring a realm that I should never cross. An area that most people never think about or better yet, would never tell and would take to their grave if questioned. I believe like most, I'm only looking at this situation objectively and not with fortitude to further explore in any way. But I must because I have to be certain of how much of my prison has been given away without my knowledge or consent. I know I've held my prison in check and I've never even allowed it to surface in the presence of my family and dearest friends. But here and now I can't look away to what can happen if I don't put an end to this dilemma that I've carried with me for more than half my life. I bury my face in my hands and slowly rock back and forth with the conviction of knowing that I might have done something that I can't prove has never happened. I keep telling myself, assuring myself that this has never happened and that I've given into thoughts that were just investigations of all angles of possibility. I sit still embracing the silence and trying not to think of anything more. For a brief moment there is nothing, nothing but a faint breathing which is my own. Slowly I come to my senses, hoping I never have to experience a moment of torture such as this one. My head begins to pound and I know this is something of a serious matter because I rarely experience headaches. I sit still again to allow my body to absorb the throbbing and try to relax. It's amazing how my body starts to readjust. As I regain my faculties, the throbbing slowly dissipates and subsides slowly with every other beat. However my reflection won't stop there. It must continue through until it ends. Meantime I must collect, analyze, hypothesize and find possible solutions even if they are not true. So my subconscious leads me to one exchange I've avoided and have only dealt with on the surface; my niece.

But as I do this I look further into how I've attempted to pass on this disease, my prison onto my niece. So she is not from the main chain of the family and is more of a far extension if you posted this information on a family tree. This is my reasoning that I've fought with in allowing my prison to convince me that my niece should be the one. She would be the one who could carry on this legacy of mine and endure me with exchanges of my own prison. I stop again and wonder what is wrong with me to entertain thoughts as these? I reason with myself that this is my niece and for a long stupor I've been torn between giving her my prison and protecting her from my prison.

But alas, I don't know how to turn it (my prison) off or better yet find an alter ego of it that I can substitute. Even in doing such a thing (turning it off) I don't think substitution will have a long term effect. That goes the same for stopping my prison altogether, just shutting it off. I've been down this road before as I've tried to stop my prison in the past, but here I am again, devising another plan. I don't think I can do that, the shutting down thing, I've had it for too long and it will take just as long to get rid of it. That would mean the rest of my life from this moment forward that I would be free. But again, I've nurtured this entity of mine, this extension of myself, my pet, something that belongs to me and only me and no one, no one, could ever take it away from me.

It would mean just being a regular person, just me. This is where in certain situations that my prison has helped me to play along in the games that are played between male and females. All my life as far back as I can remember, my prison has played a part in how I've dealt with conversations with females. Whether good or bad, my prison has encouraged me with confidence with every encounter with a female. However, I haven't pursued every encounter with a female into something more than just friendly conversation, but the idea of innuendoes is bit arousing depending on the female company. Besides it's a challenge just to see how far you and your competitor can push one another before mistakenly going over the edge and revealing what are their true intentions; teasing.

This curse I have, my prison, when it was initiated, it was the start of what I now consider the curse of my life. I often tell myself the old adage, "…you never forget your first. You can't always remember those thereafter, but the first…" For this I pursue my life under a cloak of disguise. I lead a life of parallel people, the cursed one and the one with morals who is trying to break away from the other. Yet these two facades of me are dependent upon the other for existence. See the moral one can be approached by a potential victim unknowing that the cursed one is looking for the right opportunity to pounce. But once the cursed one has attempted to implore its infection, the moral one is shown the effects of what has occurred and is left to promote healing.

Prostration

When I arrived that morning, there was a note on my desk that an unscheduled meeting was to take place at nine thirty. I wasn't sure what would be the subject since as a company everything seemed to go well the past Friday. I mean there weren't any deadlines that were missed, no one had any discrepancies that warranted attention and besides when I was leaving that day people seemed to be in a good mood. So this meeting at the last minute was unexpected and piqued my curiosity.

As the timeframe drew, I decided to be in the meeting some twenty minutes earlier. I could get the best seat to be in position for what was to come. My Manager was one who did not play with sentimental arrangements. He was right to the point; whatever it was he had to say to the staff.

I sat there quietly trying to figure out what was the rush for this particular meeting. That's when I could hear footsteps and mumbled conversations growing closer to the door of the conference room. There was my cubicle buddy and another guy I knew from the other department. The two of them were acting as if they were buddies from a long past. I paid no attention until the two of them tried to engage me with talk about the new additions in personnel…again. I didn't entertain them and they left me alone.

Before our manager walked in everyone else involved in the meeting were stepping through the door. We all made greetings and our manager sat. He went around the conference table asking everyone to give a brief description of themselves as to where they fit within the company. Of course some tried to elevate their status which prompted a chuckle around the room.

Then our manager began with the announcement of the new contract we were awarded after hours on the past Friday and into sometime Saturday. We were all excited about the award and the dialogue began. Our manager stopped us and proceeded with detailed assignments because in order to complete the project we had to allow the client to review our work daily along the way. In addition we had to work in smaller teams within a section with more than one acting manager. We all understood the new layout for smaller teams being the largest of the assignment tiers. So our manager's assistant began passing out the team assignments when I received mine. I looked twice, paused, looked it over and caught the attention of the assistant manager for the oversight. She explained that there was no mistake because she handpicked the teams based on past performance and knowledge. She went on to say that my team was included within her other teams for continuity. I didn't argue but just smiled because I was a lead and that meant I was given the authority to make sound decisions. However when I looked again at my teammate I didn't recognize the name. I asked the assistant manager who was this person and was this person here in the meeting. She snickered at me because I realize the joke was on me. You see if I would've listen to my colleague I would've known that the lady sitting across from me was the new girl. My assistant manager continued with after reviewing the new girl's resume and speaking with previous employers, she discovered how well versed she was in experience and that she would do well for this project. However, she needed to be teamed with someone who had previous experienced in this line of work, so I was chosen. My interpretation; I did have the qualifications, however I was chosen for this team and my teammate because I was also married and she was single, hah!

My colleague looked up and whispered, "If you need any help, ask me first, okay?"

I nodded with an acknowledgement and tried to listen in on my manager as he tried to explain the other guidelines required for the project. While I looked on, I caught a slight wave out the corner of my eye. My new teammate wanted to speak with me after the meeting. The meeting didn't drag on like I expected and that was a relief. As we started to file out of the conference room, my colleague grabbed me by my arm and nodded with a wink and a sly smile. I tried to dismiss his gesture and informed him I would catch him later for lunch.

I waited outside the conference room for my teammate; she held a conversation with our assistant manager. It appeared as if they knew I was waiting and decided to continue talking. I felt like a child waiting outside the principal's office for a disciplinary decision. Finally she came out and introduced herself, I the same and she asked me where I sat. I gave her the location and she explained that she was on the other side of the floor and that's what she was talking about with the assistant manager. She said that our assistant manager was moving the both us temporary into an office space that included a large drawing table because our task was the second to be looked over.

I tried not to look over her physical attributes as a male I'm prone to do so recklessly. She decided to walk a step ahead of me. As I looked her over one more time, I tried to remember but I knew I was past my second, my prison tapped me ever so nicely on my shoulder. Not to be embarrassed by the notion, I took a long stride caught her pace and slightly past her. As I glanced over to alert her of my location, she held back a smile.

We sat briefly in my cubicle discussing her background and mine. I didn't realize that we had followed some of the same paths in pursuing this line of work. Then we discussed the project, the hours estimated to finish and our plan to accomplish this task. She offered several ideas some of which we were consider for the project and I started a running file of points to address once we moved.

I started to input some of this information in my laptop when I noticed the time, it was lunchtime. I asked was she going to catch up with some friends here and she said she doesn't know anyone enough to have lunch with them. Dammit. So I tried to present myself as an honorable man and offered to have lunch with her if she didn't mind. She accepted and asked me where was a good place to eat. I didn't have a clue because I wasn't prepared for her reaction. So I asked her what her type of cuisine. She explained that she did like "hole-in-the-wall" type of settings. I had a place in mind and told her it was time to leave. She had to get her coat, so I told her I would meet her in the lobby by the elevator.

"…let's play?"

My colleague met me before I got there, he was with his new teammate and we started to talk about the project. His teammate noticed the elevator doors opening and started to step in, my colleague offered to continue our conversation inside. I stopped him and said I was waiting for my teammate. The both of them snickered and just before the elevator doors closed, my colleague's teammate mentioned that I was trying to keep her to myself and the doors closed.

We had a nice, funny time at lunch. I discovered through various subjects that she was about five years younger than me. I avoided as many personal subjects as I could, but she persisted. She asked about my family and wanted to see pictures. I showed her the ones I had in my wallet and she made comments on each. That's when the waitress approached us and asked me did I want dessert, I said no, but she then asked my teammate with the assumption of being my wife. My teammate didn't falter and explained since I wasn't; she wasn't and thanked the waitress. I looked at her to find any discomfort, she looked at me and explained that we were sitting together laughing and joking so the waitress just assumed after looking at your hand.

As we entered the building which housed our company, she thanked me by hugging me. I replied that she would do the same for me. She said yes with a smile. We entered the elevator with several other people from different floors and the elevator was soon crowded. My teammate moved to let others in, but she moved closer to my side until she wound up standing in front of me. She barely backed up into me and my prison wanted to rise to the occasion. I moved slightly away and nearly bumped a man standing behind me. He gave me a stare of caution and I obliged.

I started to feel a rise of my prison and fought to quench it. My teammate must of felt something about me cause she looked up over her shoulder to tell me that she will find a place for us tomorrow to enjoy for lunch. I tried not to lean forward to acknowledge, instead I said I would try to pick the most expensive place I could think of in the downtown area.

This was the type of exchange we kept from that point forward. Our relationship grew into friendly jostling of words, quips and looks. Many people at the job thought that we made a good team. My colleague however was a bit jealous and sought every opportunity to become involved when he could. It wasn't his character but he was single, I was married and he couldn't understand how a nice looking woman would feel comfortable around me. It was such that he would schedule meetings with me and my teammate along with his to discuss the next step of our work. It was a bit confusing at times because our work and his work weren't on the same time frame nor were we doing the exact same thing.

Eventually my colleague's teammate intervened to limit our meetings but he persisted until my teammate made an observation that she thought he liked her. I said no he was jealous of our relationship. She said from day one she knew he would be trouble and that she didn't like his demeanor. We both laughed at what we both knew were true.

Once again our relationship took another turn. My teammate wanted to stay late to finish certain parts of the project. I obliged but I started to notice that on some occasions, we would be the last to leave. She eventually started to make certain that I inform my wife of my working late, or better yet, she started to remind me that I should call my wife if I didn't. This started to concern me because one night while leaving, I found out that she lived in the downtown area and she asked me if I could drive her home. I explained that by the time I get my car from the garage and drive her home she would already be there. She agreed and we walked the six blocks.

We talked the entire way concerning many subjects but the one we seemed to connect on was her playing field hockey. I could only relate it to football, hockey or soccer. She explained how when she was young, her mother pushed her into the sport because of how she enjoyed the games of contact that other girls didn't enjoy. So her mother would take her to practice then leave her to take her sisters to ballet, girl scouts or some other non-contact sport. I laughed. She explained that was how she developed such strong and muscular legs. I agreed. She said that the sport did provide her with travel and through that she was able to collect posters from other places. She went on to say that she decorated a portion of her apartment with some of those experiences.

We were finally at her apartment building and talked briefly before I started to say my goodbye. That's when she offered me the opportunity to come and see her place. I explained that it was late and that I'd better leave to get home so that I could be ready for our inspection from our client. She accepted but wanted a rain check and that she was going to cash in on soon. As I left she held her arms out for a hug. I walked to her and whispered goodbye. As I said this, she lightly kissed me on the check and thanked me for all I've done to make her feel comfortable in the company. I never moved during her kiss and when she finished I slowly backed away, ignoring what she just did, smirked and said that she better be ready tomorrow.

When I arrived home everyone was upstairs and I heard my wife yell to me. I removed my coat and shoes and carried my shoes upstairs to my bedroom. My wife was sitting on the bed with a lounging outfit of loose thin pants and the women's version of an A-line t-shirt. Her hair was somewhat out of place and she appeared as if she had just awakened from sleep. I changed into my boxers, moved into the bathroom to freshen up and returned. She didn't acknowledge my presence at first, but with her back toward me she asked me how long would this project last. I explained the time schedule and she turned to look at me. I was waiting for her to say something when she said that I was working too hard and asked me if she could help me to relax. Her timing could not be perfect and I moved closer to her as she brought me joy, relief and a way to remove my connection with my prison.

Through the course of the project, my teammate continued to befriend me in ways that I had trouble deciphering. For example, on occasion she would bring in lunch or even dinner for us to share. She began touching me on the shoulders, on my back and once slapped me on my butt once after we found out in a meeting that we were ahead of schedule. Her actions were uncomfortable but tolerated, because she kept my mind off of other things that would excite my prison and allowed me to enjoy the fruits of my labor with my understanding wife. So I ignored her way of expression toward our relationship until we were called into a meeting.

In this meeting we were both told that we were being transferred temporary to another team because they were behind on their portion of the project. It was good and bad to hear the news. I would not have my teammate to myself which meant fewer lunches together and no more home cooked meals.

We established a good rapport with our new teammates and continued to work as much as we could together. However, the new female teammate began to pull my teammate from me and I was left with the other female who was not much on socializing. I dealt with the circumstances and we continued to work well as a whole.

Our manager had announced that through this first phase of work our client was so please at the work our company was doing for them that they gave us the entire project and the future one. He also announced a celebration party this coming Friday right after work. As usual my teammate made certain I told my wife.

The time had arrived and my manager had coordinated taxis for the entire company and off we went to rented banquet hall of an expensive restaurant downtown. We drank, partied and danced the night away. It was a good time but with all things an end has to come. Before I announced that I was leaving to my teammate, I was approached but my new female teammate who too was leaving. So we decided to leave together.

"…let's play?"

As we left to await a taxi the new teammate began to talk about how she noticed my teammate and I interacting and she wasn't sure what was really going on between us. I tried to explain but she continued and that's when the taxi arrived. When we got in, the driver asked us where we were going. I informed the driver of the address of my company. My new teammate explained that she didn't have a car and asked me if I could drive her home from our company. It was good she made that request because she was becoming sleepy from her drinking. I tried to ignore this so as to not give the driver the wrong impression of us.

As we now stood in the elevator, my new teammate began to lean up against me for support. I held her to my side and asked if she was alright. She looked up at me and said she would need some help home. I told her my car was right near the elevator and to hold on to me. I got her into the car and she gave me her address before nodding off to sleep.

When we arrived, I woke her and offered to help her to her door. She said she would like that because she couldn't keep her balance. I got her out of the car, up the steps to her apartment, entered her apartment and place her on her couch. That's when she felt like she was going to vomit. I went to the bathroom and found a trash can. When I came back into the living room, she was just about to place her hands over her mouth. She let go with a force that meant she either drank too much or ate the wrong thing.

In her effort to expel the unwanted material, she spilled some on her clothes. Now in my opinion this was awkward and I had to figure out how to not get myself into more trouble. She looked down at herself, said something, looked up at me and apologized. Her breathe was not welcoming but I asked her would she be alright left alone. She reached out to me and asked me to stay a while. Trying to be a gentleman, I decided to stay. I helped her to the bathroom and shut the door for her to take care of herself. It seemed like forever and when she returned she was in a robe. Now my prison tapped me and I tried to ignore it. She again apologized and asked me if I would stay a little longer I said yes.

We sat on her couch and she sat there with her legs propped

up next to her on the couch. She turned on the television and we sat there making small talk. My new teammate soon felt the need to lean up against me. As time passed so did the resistance of my arm and it started to ache. So I raised it and she slid into the pit of my arm. She pulled herself closer as if she was cold. So we sat some more as she flicked through the channels and finally settling on one. We watched whatever it was while I thought about what I should do and what I wanted to do with her. Again she looked up at me to thank me but this time she pushed herself up to move closer to my face. Then the new teammate moved her arm that wasn't under my arm and reached out to hold my face. I looked at her and she pulled me closer to thank me again. I could smell the mouthwash on her breath which was a good thing and then she kissed me, with succulent lips and even gave me some tongue. I didn't know how to react, but the kiss was good. When the new teammate pulled away she apologized for her actions. I forgave her and explained my dedication. She stopped me and explained that I was one of the better guys in the office and for a moment she hoped…I stopped her and explained it could happen but it could never be cause of my commitment.

Something inside me wanted but another wasn't even feeling the moment. Don't get me wrong, she is pretty and from what I can tell, she has a nice body, and our conversations are okay thus far, but…Besides during this entire moment, my prison was nowhere to be found. In some way I was happy about that but was saddened by the fact that this was a glimpse of an opportunity that would never happen.

We sat there for a long time, my new teammate, still under my arm, me still holding her, and the two of us evaluating the words we want to say to one another. I broke the ice by telling her that I hope she finds the guy she deserves and I'm sorry I'm not the one for her and finally, that what has happened here tonight was something I'm not ready to share with anyone. She nodded shamefully, but I added that I respect her and will make every effort to continue our friendship and working relationship. I waited for her to flip what I was saying back on me, but she didn't. She just snuggled a little more under my arm and we watched the television. Eventually she started to fall asleep and I fought mine. She offered the couch, but I said I should go and would see her on Monday. As I opened the door to leave she sauntered up to me, thanked me again, and reached out to hug me. I leaned over to do the same and she kissed me again on the lips. Again I didn't stop her and when she finished, she touched me on the face and said she would see me Monday. As I left I knew our relationship would not be the same, but a tolerated fabrication of what she wanted. I did congratulate myself for realizing I wasn't a bad guy after all.

Monday morning rolled around and the conversations were in full swing about the gathering on Friday. I enjoyed listening to many of the accusations and mannerisms of some of my coworkers, even the managers. I laughed some and made some small comments as I made my way to office. I didn't see either of my teammates and started to work. Some time had passed and I started to become concerned about my teammates.

Eventually my new teammate showed up and we began talking about the party, avoiding our encounter as much as possible. As we started working she noticed that both our teammates hadn't showed up for work. Over time as the next hour passed, my new teammate went on the search for our teammates. She too would be gone for a while, so I continued my work.

Just before lunchtime, my new teammate returned with a concerned look on her face. I inquired and she got up to close the office door. She went on in a frantic behavior about how our teammates went to an after party at one of our coworkers and wound up sleeping with two of the guys here at work. As stupid as it sounded I asked were they involved in a swinger's event. She said no, that each was involved with one person at different times, she didn't know, but she did know that it didn't occur in the same place. I wasn't sure it what she explained was a relief, but I did know that I needed to do some investigating.

To my dissatisfaction it turned out to be my colleague and

my teammate. I knew he wanted her but to disgrace her like that was uncalled. I returned to my office where and I found my teammates, all of them. I asked them if they needed to take the day off, since I was still the lead and informed them that we were on schedule.

    We didn't take lunch together or at the same times. I stayed back trying to digest all of the past few days. I was happy that my home life was steady and there weren't any signs of trouble. That's when my colleague knocked on the door. He wanted to know if I was going to lunch. I passed on the possible offer and he seemed awkward about what to talk about next. I said nothing because I already knew but he didn't know this information. He paused and said he would talk to me later and left. That talk never happened and I never said that I knew.

    For the most part things returned to normal and my teammate and I were eventually removed from assisting the other team and was back to our part of the project. It took some time; eventual late nights, laughter again and some touching on the shoulders. It took a while but my teammate eventually told me of what happened that night. I asked her why she would tell me. She explained that she liked me and she didn't want to ruin my marriage but she would have given anything for just one night. I told my teammate that I was flattered but inquired as to why one night. She tried to explain her bad or off and on relationships and that she had never felt as comfortable with me as she did with anyone before me. I tried to dismiss what she was trying to tell me but she continued with she just wanted to see what it would feel like and she started to apologize. I stopped my teammate and grabbed her to hug her before she started to cry. She sobbed softly and when she finished, I kissed her passionately. She responded and got more involved. I had to slowly stop her.

    My teammate sat back down in her chair and tried to explain that she became a bit jealous that I took home the other teammate and she wanted me to take her home. I told her that I wanted to leave because I was tired. She went on to say that she then started to drink more and our other teammate she was getting close with asked her to join her at one of the manger's home for a little after party. So they did and she started to lose focus when she saw my colleague who was also drunk. So the two of them played with the notion and eventually ended up sleeping together. She asked me not to judge her and I said I wouldn't but wanted to make certain that she wasn't pregnant or contracted something. She said no.

In the weeks or months that followed we eventually finished the project and started working on our own projects and that's when I learned that all three women had accepted jobs with other companies. I heard our managers tried to offer other incentives besides some additional pay, but they all declined at different times. It hurt because they were nice people and I thought we were working on what had happened that night at the work celebration, but I realized how important a woman's reputation is to them.

As I thought about this, in comes my colleague to engage me about the leaving of my teammates. I talked about them and he just couldn't wait to tell me what happened that night with my now old teammate. I asked how it started between them. He said she showed up at the manager's house and eventually started drinking. He said he finally had a chance to talk with her. He said as they talked my name came up on several different subjects. My now old teammate went on about this and that about me to the point where my colleague said to her that she should look elsewhere. He tried to say after that she was all over him and that's how it happened. I just listened and added here or there. After he had said all that he could in elevating the matter he asked me my opinion of if he should pursue her. I said I couldn't tell him. Our conversation started to sour and he said he would catch up with me later.

On the way home I got a call from my wife explaining she would be late coming home and that the kids went to a summer league game. I asked if I should swing by and picked them up, she said no that they had a ride. So home I arrived and I sat there thinking about my behavior in all this that occurred at work. I felt bad because I allowed my working relationships to become skew with a personal or lustful relationship. I even led my colleague into revengeful behavior because I tried to ignore his pursuit of my now old teammate. I even thought about why those women had been planning for so long to leave. I wanted to find a way to punish myself for not being as aware and finding a way to offset all of this.

That's when my wife came in the door. She yelled for me because I had all the lights our and was sitting on the chase chair after having my second drink. She followed my voice and reached for the lights, I stopped her. She asked me if I was comfortable. I said yes but that she should get comfortable. I was prepared to somehow have this conversation of my concern with her. I could hear her movements toward me and I sat with no motion. She reached out toward me and I touched her hand. She asked if she could sit with me. I slid back in the chase chair and awaited her to find a place to sit with me. Instead she grabbed my legs, turning them upright and slid over them until she was sitting over my manhood. I rose with excitement and before I could move, she started on my pants. I twitched and wiggled until she got my pants, my boxers and my shoes off. I was just amazed. I felt her slide up to my manhood and that's when I noticed that she kept her skirt on and nothing else underneath.

Our moment was filled with relief comfort and understanding. I could feel that she understood what I was going through at work and that I had time to figure it out, to fix it the best way I could. I ignored everything after that thought crossed my mind. However, I had a new task to work on. The next day my wife came to me in our bedroom with the dress she had on the previous night. There was a smeared stain on it that had already caused discoloration to the two toned dress. I tried to explain but she held up her hand and said that the only way to appease her was to take her shopping for two dresses, one similar to the one she held up and a new one to make her feel better.

Detestation

Ever since the party I've noticed a change in my uncle's behavior. He seems to avoid me as if I have a plague or something. It bothers me to see him uncomfortable around me. He looks like a whimp, always making up excuses not to stay in my company. I have a problem with that type of attitude. It's not like neither one of us has an idea of what the other is thinking. For example, the first time was the weirdest. As soon as I came down the stairs, I could feel, I mean he's always noticed me since I've been here and sometimes he can't take his eyes off of me.

If you could see me! I mean I'm not bragging, but I've been told that I have a model's face. My eyes make me seem so innocent and I always add just a hint of makeup. I discovered that trick at the mall. But my lips are a great compliment, they're full but not too big and I keep the lip gloss on them. I like to make them look pouty or as if I'm out of breathe, panting-like. Other times I've been told that I don't look my age. That's because with my short style hair (I have shoulder length hair but I'm a little lazy in the up keep) gives me just enough of a boyish look and I can managed this length. Once I had my hair frizzled and I looked as if I'd just gotten out of the shower. I was even told that I looked foreign, can you believe it? Whatever. But it goes well with my skin tone that isn't too light or too dark, like a lightened caramel color.

What's more interesting is that I have a nice body. It's not big up top, but below is, well, to the fellas, they can't keep their eyes off it. It doesn't just stop there; I have the calves to match. Yes my body is proportioned from the waist down. My lower half is not that big compared to my upper half where it would seem that I have to very different body types. I don't help my cause by making all of what I have worked. Yeah that part of me, I make it seem natural like I was born to make my bottom do what it does. But to have such a body and a face like mine is unheard of. That's a weird thought when you're coming out of a high school with your girlfriends sometimes carrying your books for you. They think that being around me will get them the chance that I get from the fellas. But I have to admit with my eyes, my hair, my bottom and my legs; it's hard not to salivate. However, I wish I had more upstairs to giggle about or when I have on a shirt with no bra. Now that really turns them on! And to make the package (that's me) look even better, I've never worn clothes that matches my age. It's no wonder my uncle's friends haven't' looked at me the way he does. I know this because I know I look good.

I'm not really sure when I became aware of how good I look. Maybe it was when my brothers, my sister and I were with my cousins and those boys kept following us around. Hmm, I remember that because one of my brothers got upset and wanted to say something to them. It was a good thing that my parents approached us from the other street and this scared the boys off. What made it more interesting is that they found us again later, only my cousins, my sister and I didn't have our brothers with us. Man they were so interested in us. They were encircling us asking us questions like how old we were, are we mixed, where did we get the nice clothes and how our clothes made us look so pretty. But that's all they did, talk, talk and more talk. None of them could take us out anywhere or buy even a Popsicle for us.

Nah, it didn't happened then, let me see, it was probably earlier when we use to get our hair done in a group as if we were going to go somewhere when our moms were finished. They would play in our hair, hold our faces in their hands and tell us to look in the mirror and notice all of the features in our faces which made us beautiful. They showed us how when we grew up we too could have bodies like theirs and so on. Those made me feel so good. It was as if they knew all the secrets to being pretty and nice looking and, and, beautiful.

I do think I'm beautiful because I can see it every time I look in the mirror or when some guy looks me over and just can't look away. That's when I know I've got him where I want him. You know I can get him to do some things for me. He has to prove to me that he's worthy of my beauty in his presence. What he would get is a girl who knows her way around sports, a little, a girl who dresses well and one who has a good disposition. See, I would know how to act in front of his boys and the jealous girls, but he better not play me like I'm stupid or something. It's just that simple, I can bring him favor and at the same time all the other guys would be jealous of him being with me. Or I can bring him embarrassment and then not only will none of the other girls touch him; the guys will mock him as one who couldn't hold onto me. The other desperate girls would now be his catch.

Oh and the girls would just have to suck it up. All the talk they would do would only say to me and even to them that they wish that they were in my position. They would have to have something close to a total package. But even then, they couldn't handle the pressure that comes with being a beaut like me.

It's this body that I now have that is so attractive to the guys. I can wear anything, and I mean anything, and it would look good on me, anything. I think this was why my cousin ripped my bathing suit at the pool party. He wanted to see just as much as the other guys. You know, sometimes I ask myself if my cousin likes me in some way. I mean I've been around him since we were kids and he use to play a lot more with me, my sister and his sisters. It can't be because I've grown up in all the right areas. I've beat out my sister and my younger cousin in those areas! They are both so small up top but I think they're trying to catch me in the bottom area.

My cousin's older sister, she's a little bit different. She knows how to move, what to say and when to say it. I must admit I'm a little jealous of her but she poses no threat. I mean even at the party that night when the guys were all over me, she was the only one that stayed on the sidelines. Once when I looked in her direction, she wasn't even looking my way. It looked to me as if she had met her match and just gave in. I think she's a bit strange if you ask me, but that's my cousin for you. But my other cousin, she's one that I will have to keep an eye on. This one knows how to move, what to say and she can put on these expressions that seem to mesmerize guys. I mean like at the pool party she had her own little group of guys and girls, mainly guys. But this group seems to be one that, well they seem like they're up to something I just can't place yet. Her group talks mainly amongst themselves,

~ 145 ~

but the girls on the group look good. But again, my cuz can't compete. Yeah she does have a little more up top than me and I have a little more than her below and yes she can fit my pants, but she can't do it like me. My cousin can move and she can really dance which makes what she has look even better, but who wants a sweating girl all over you?

But my cousin, he talks with me and now and then he plays with me but he seems afraid to touch me, I mean anywhere. He's just as nervous as my uncle. Hunh, I know if he did touch me in a wrong way, he would want another touch either right then and there or later on. And that touch would lead to many more touches. Yeah that's why he stays at a distance. He's not like his other friends, like the one at the party who stood there trying to get the best look at me when I lost half my bathing suit bottom. I still don't see why he (my cousin) did it instead of the other guy, I think he was just a distant friend of my cousin, but he kept touching himself across his stomach and licking his lips when I would look in his direction. I knew he just couldn't wait to have a moment alone with me. He couldn't handle me, he's just a child playing in a man's game trying to look and act like a man. What I need is an older man, one who is more experienced and who could show me things that those boys just can't. I want them old but not too old in age like my grandfather or someone, weird.

I just can't see my uncle teaching me something like that. Now that just seems...I don't want to even talk about it. But it was nice to see him looking in my direction as if he had other intentions, until he gets caught. It was like that moment in time when he brushed up against me at the putt-putt. He started getting rather close, so I bumped him to get him off me. How was I to know I'd lose my balance? But I felt...anyway I didn't feel right afterwards and I didn't want that to happen again with him. But he's my uncle and I do care a lot about him. He's been there just as much as my dad. I could talk with him on some subjects but boy would he get uncomfortable when he had to discuss guys and girls together in any fashion. He did the same thing with his own girls.

But there was another time when my cousins and I were

talking in my room and my uncle knocked on the door to enter before he was allowed. Boy, were my cousins scrambling for cover and I couldn't grab anything. I was so embarrassed. Well my uncle first opened the door and then stepped in halfway to announce that we should be getting ready for...I can't remember. Anyway, as he looked us over, I could tell he was looking me over with more, more, interest. You know when a guy is looking in one direction then starts to look in another but you're in between both looks, so he looks you over as he going to look in that other direction? All I had on was a teddy styled top and some brief styled shorts. But I didn't have on a bra and my shorts were just right. After he said what he said and left, I looked down, over my shirt and that's when I could see that my girls were protruding and with a little enthusiasm. Now if I could see them from my position, just imagine what he saw. At that point I wanted to call him a pervert, but it made me mad to think of him in such a way. Well after that incident I decided to avoid him some and to dress a little differently when I know he is around.

At the family gathering I didn't see much of my uncle once we got there. Maybe he was looking at our other relatives along with the other perverted men in my family. That's the only part I hate about my family, there's always one or two that want to hug up on you, tell you to prance around so that they can get a good look at you because you're growing so fast and then stare for a bit. Then afterwards they try to compare you with other female relatives in the family. Some of the other female relatives vie for this attention, crazy.

But when I did see my uncle he seemed preoccupied with his cousin. Those two are like brothers and I'm not certain, but I know if my uncle acts like that, then his cousin must act like that also. When my uncle passed me he didn't even look my direction. It's not like I wanted him to look at me, but I've come to expect it and he didn't. I think this might be a good sign about how he's been acting since I arrived.

Vexation

My son has called on me several times to give him some help as he tried to tie his tie. I can hear him yelling and almost swearing to the fact that this is why he doesn't wear ties. I allow him to grow in anger 'cause I remembered when I had my first experience tying a tie. Meanwhile the girls are chatting up a storm in somebody's room, from where I stood, I just can't tell. In addition I could hear my wife in her closet laughing at all the noises the kids are making. She really likes the sounds. So I'm trying to finish dressing as quickly as possible and then I go assist my boy. When I arrived in the bathroom he shared with his sisters, he had at least two knots in his tie and was working on a third. For a moment I just stand there in amusement.

I step out of the bathroom for a moment to call to my wife to find out how long she will take. She steps out of her room and shows me how far she's gotten dressed. I tried to surmise a timeframe from what's she's showed me but I can't tell. I move to enter my son's room and I find him sitting on his bed working on another tie. When he sees me he looks over at me and points to several of ties I have never untied that he has used as templates from my room. I ask him which tied does he thinks goes best with his suit. We figure this out and I show him, facing him, on the mechanics of tying a tie. He gets the idea after the fourth try and I tell him to stand still because I have to retrieve something from my room. I return with a expensive fragrance and show him how and where to add this to his suit and body so that the ladies won't stop sniffing on him. Now we are ready, but the ladies aren't.

My wife has been looking forward to all of us attending this awards banquet for her best friend for at least a month. Somehow since the kids are well into their teens and my wife's friend had extra tickets, we figured we would invite them into our world of functions and visits and gatherings. The kids were overjoyed, speaking about this event to their friends building up the suspense about how important this award was for their mother's friend.

So once again my son and I waited and tried to find something sports related on the television. We could hear the ladies rejecting this, accepting that and inquiring about how this made them look like that. I joked with my son about how long their moment was going to last before we would have to leave. He laughed along with me and then we saw my two daughters coming down stairs. Aside from how handsome my son looked, my daughters were...wow. They sat down in chairs with precaution and then my niece came down just before my wife and the two of them looked just as remarkable. That being said we were finally ready to leave and we did.

At the driveway to the luxury hotel, we were met with valets and we exited the car for one of them to quickly hop into my car to drive off slowly. As we watched the car pass before us, we all stopped to look around with impression, realizing how expensive this event must be for us. I led the way into the hotel lobby with my wife on my arm as the girls filed behind along with my son bringing up the rear. As we entered we realize that there were either several parties going on or that there were a lot more people than we imagine would be here. The kids looked around with amazement hoping that none of the other patrons would look upon them as being out of place.

We moved about enjoying the ambiance which was very pleasant and I could see that the kids were becoming a little more relaxed once they saw some other kids who looked like they too were dragged into this event. Somehow they seem to meet near the deserts and the wife and I were left alone to further walk about the place. Her friend, who was a little nervous, finally caught up with us and engaged us in interesting conversation about the event. We were soon met with other friends and we all stood in place conversing back and forth, trading places as the conversation changed as if we were playing twister.

The event went along with no interruptions and we didn't have to fidget in our seats because the ceremony speeches didn't take long. As the ceremony was about to close, a crew enter from the rear of the ballroom to open up the space for more mobility. Then we were released to enjoy ourselves. It didn't take long for many of the patrons to get on the floor for a little dancing, more talking and, yes drinking.

So once again I was left alone as the little lady went off with her friend who invited us and some other friends to talk and enjoy the rest of the night. I sat there laughing at myself because again I have been left alone with my prison however the catch was I was now in public. Now how could I enjoy my prison in public and not get caught? So I played with the thought, laughing a little more to myself and sipping my drink. It all was a bit surreal because of how much I've yearned for moments of being alone like this one. Now here I am tempted and challenged to keep my prison in check while trying to enjoy it at the same time. I knew it wouldn't happen but it was nice to dream about it.

Eventually boredom started to set in and with a thump. I tried to brush it off because I've experienced this before in many instances. But for some reason the sensation held me because I realize that I really didn't know anyone here. This realization played into my boredom and I set out to combat it. What happened next that helped me to change my emotional state was what I saw. There near the end of the dancing crowd was a young man enticed into dancing with an older woman. I wasn't sure if this young man was related to this older lady or that she couldn't find a dance partner, but he seemed a little embarrassed about going through with the task. Eventually he gave in and tried to entertain the lady by imitating her movements. She stopped and whispered something to him before he started to relax and enjoy the moment. The lady moved with a different style all of her own while the young man did what young men do most, dance in a way that would entice and eventually get him close enough to the lady. She allowed his efforts in good fun and they danced about as they disappeared in and out the moving crowd.

I sat up in my seat trying not to stare in their direction as a means of entertainment. The two of them looked a little strained in their interaction and I couldn't stop looking for other clues to their relationship. I think I wanted to enjoy this moment as a method of relating it to one of my past experiences. So I used it to my advantage to indulge the effects of the many drinks, my chance at relieving boredom and to embrace more reflection.

I couldn't get away from visiting my grands and seeing my cousin. Even though we stayed at other ends of the city we stayed in touch constantly. It was unfortunate that he wasn't always in the best financial shape to come and visit me and he constantly reminded me of this fact. However, he knew I was coming and there was a chance that I would stay longer. After I arrived I wasted no time in finding my space for my clothes and headed on outside to catch up with what was happening in the neighborhood.

My cousin showed me the new kids who moved into the neighborhood and the new girls of prospect. As we mingled I notice one of the new girls that I hadn't seen before. To me she was gorgeous and at thirteen a girl like her didn't have to have a lot, physically. I found my way through the crowd to get my chance to talk with her. She didn't ignore me nor turned me away with her conversation, and I talked about this and laughed about that. She finally explained in some round about detail that she was single and I approached her with the line of the times which indicated a relationship, I asked her, "Could I stand a chance?" This line was simple and direct without being offensive. Using this line expressed to a girl that you were interested in her and she had the choice of declining without the guy succumbing to a devastating heartbreak. However, to my amazement she replied, "…but I don't know you." I was taken by the fact that she didn't say no or became offensive and she gave me a chance to explain my approach. I countered with, "But we can get to know one another, trust me." I didn't quit there and introduced myself and asked her name. Now believe it or not after all of this talking back and forth we never asked the other about a name. Again she amazed me by agreeing to my explanation and then we exchanged simple personal information.

Later into the evening my cousin had gotten the word that I was going to be this girl's boyfriend. He pulled me out of the crowd and inquired how I pulled off getting her to be my girlfriend. My cousin explained that he too was interested in her a little but he never pursued the idea. But he was happy for me because he explained that the girl had other suitors who had failed and some miserably.

Well many in the neighborhood eventually found out that this girl and me were a couple in puppy love and to not disturb. Some of the guys around my age told me how displeased they were in the girl's decision to pick me. Often they would engage me to a point of fighting. But I kept my cool because this girl made me feel special and what I would've done and tried to do have now changed.

Because of this act and many others, my girlfriend was so intrigued with me and so interested in me that I didn't have to do much to impress her. It wasn't that we weren't on the same level intellectually or other, but she liked simplicity and that was a plus to a young with limited finances. On the other hand I didn't hesitate to find ways to make her happy, keep her happy. She spoke of the two us in the future being married with kids living the high life. At this point my prison never showed up and we had a great time together. I was becoming so involved with this girl that I decided to stay the rest of the summer with my grands. My mother even approved of this action telling my grandmother that she hoped that this girl would keep my attention and my behavior in check.

All was going well until the day my aunt noticed me leaving to go visit my girlfriend. She stopped me before I descended the porch steps and explained that my relationship wasn't going to last. I was offended and lashed back at her telling her how nice and beautiful this girl was compared to her. She laughed at me and reiterated her fact. I didn't know what else to say to her so I tried to just dismiss the ordeal. But again before I could leave the presence of my aunt she reached out, grabbed my arm and pulled me close to whisper to me. What she said to me shocked me and made me scared. She said to me that she would tell my girlfriend that we <u>were playing</u> and how much I enjoyed <u>playing</u> with her. I pulled away and at first I wanted to run to tell my girlfriend before my aunt would but then I realized that my girlfriend wouldn't believe me. So I paused and begged my aunt to reconsider and asked her what I could do to prevent her from doing this to me. She smirked and laughed in my face until she could see the anger forming in face. My patience was wearing thin because she waited for a long time before answering. My aunt explained that she really didn't know what I could do to prevent this from happening. I started to beg again until my grandmother came to the door and asked us to keep the down the noise. My aunt giggled and thought long about what I could do as a compromise. I sat down in one of the porch chairs and waited for her response. She took so long that I started to beg again until she told me to keep down my pleading. My heart started to palpitate, at least this is how I felt, and I started to shake nervously. My aunt could see my anxiety and continued to murmur to herself as if she was having a conversation with herself about what could I do for her. As time seemed to labor I conjured in my mind the breakup between my girlfriend and me after she found this out about me. Because I started to feel this loss, tears of disappointment started to fill my eyes. I tried to look away from my aunt as she continued her contemplation. This is when I realized how much I cared about my girlfriend and to what desperate actions I was willing to take on to please her. My aunt figured this and motioned for me to lean closer to her again. I leaned over trying to hold back my tears. She waited for me to look into her eyes and she asked…"…let's play?" Her question didn't make me flinch, it only annoyed me because I hadn't been at my grands but for most of one day and here she is asking already. I asked her when she wanted to do the act and she said now. I responded in shock because I knew we couldn't pull it off without alarming our grands or someone else in the house. My aunt persisted that we had to play now or the deal was off. So I sat back in my chair and thought about the deal for a moment. She too sat back and waited for me to consider. All I could think about was my girlfriend finding out and seeing her pain and how she would be so disappointed in me. The feeling made me so numb and yet here I had to do this for my aunt or else she was going to tell on me.

I waited for my aunt to go upstairs and prepare. I sat in the porch chair and tried to wait until she would become upset with me and maybe give up on the moment. But I knew she would somehow come back downstairs like she did once before and threaten me to come upstairs. So I made my way past my grandfather while my grandmother was in the kitchen. He never blinked an eye as I passed by him. Upstairs I could hear my aunt shuffling in the sheets waiting in anticipation. As I walked to the door I couldn't bring myself to going through with this act. For some reason going through with the act was depressing and I started to feel a little nausea. I could faintly hear my aunt whispering in a hard voice for me to hurry up. I entered the room and I could see her form under the sheets. She had her legs up and held the sheet tightly up to her neck. I took my time taking off my sneakers, then my pants. My aunt started to giggle in a soft voice. The only other items I removed were my underwear and my t-shirt. I decided to keep my undershirt on. I moved to get under the sheets and asked my aunt to move over for space. She moved with a flop and looked at me with and unsettling look. My aunt demanded for me to hurry up. So after I got under the sheets she rolled over on top of me and reached under herself to find my manhood. As with precision she moved without hesitation, doing all that she could to get the arousal out of me. When she finally got what she wanted, she went after me as if she had never eaten in her life. All of her bouncing, rotation and grabbing only pissed me off more. I had grown tired of her antics and during our moment I could only think about my girl and me. I tried to block out the entire moment with my aunt and think more of the pleasant walk my girl and I had just the other day. Meanwhile my aunt continued her onslaught of self-pleasure until I had trouble keeping my arousal. She stopped and looked at me asking me to inquire what was wrong. I apologized and mentally worked myself up again for her. Then she smiled, kissed me on each of my cheeks and then laid her head in my chest. For a while I could not fathom the time that elapsed for her to finish. It seemed as if she didn't want to let go and was looking for some sort of personal record. This made me more irritated because I had to mentally challenge myself to stay firm. Eventually I felt as if I was becoming raw and I wanted her to stop. She explained in a low voice that she wanted me to release like I did on my first time. I started to plead a little to her to hurry up or we would get caught. She dismissed the thought and said to me that if I didn't she would stay here. I'm not sure how much longer we went, but I gave her the best performance I could give her to make her believe I'd release. When she realized my intention, she stopped to watch me and I could see her smiling. Afterwards she made some long sighs, and then my aunt just laid there on my chest and started to kiss me on my chest as a thank you. I presumed she didn't care if she was actually kissing my undershirt. I laid there disgusted and I felt filthy as usual and I wanted to get away. I asked her how long we were going to stay here. She explained as long as it took for me to release. Shocked I tried to assure her I did, so she felt under herself to determine my fact. She pulled her hand up to her nose and sniffed for a few seconds to determine if this were true. I'm glad that she couldn't tell and she believed me. That's when I asked her could I get up. At first she said no then she slowly moved over and I jumped up to grab my clothes. My aunt thanked me again and explained that she wasn't satisfied yet so our deal was off. I'm sure that my hate of her could be seen and she just snickered at me. Before I left I asked her how long would we have to "play" before our deal would be final. She said she wasn't sure and I wanted to beg her for a number of times before she would agree. I started not to mention that alternative but she heard me and explained to me that since I mentioned that then she would just continue our arrangement until she got tired of me or if my cousin would take my place. It hurt me so bad to have to make a choice between sacrificing my cousin or me. Since I couldn't choose I agreed to her terms until she was satisfied. She explained that she would see me either tonight or tomorrow morning.

I left the room wanting to cry and feeling betrayed once again as to making a deal and my aunt not following through on her part. In the bathroom cleaning up I thought to myself of how I got myself into this situation. The entire ordeal continually sickened me and I just didn't know what to do. I mean if I told, even now, who would believe me? So after I cleaned and dressed again I left the bathroom to go see my girlfriend.

As I walked toward my girlfriend's house, I kept checking myself for any odor that I didn't remove from the moment with my aunt. So far there was nothing I could find but as I got closer I became nervous about how to explain to my girlfriend of my lateness. I couldn't put together an alibi fast enough and it seemed as if my legs would not stop but instead moved faster toward her house. I paused at her front door before I knocked.

Immediately my girlfriend knew something was wrong with me and I didn't know how to tell her for fear of losing her. She pressed me hard about my avoidance and I held strong on not telling her. We spent the next hour or hours, going back and forth over what were wrong with me or changing the subject for a moment and going right back to my problem. Eventually our afternoon to begin exploring beyond our kissing and touching ended. Before she asked me to leave she explained that there was something I was hiding from her and that she needed to feel that she could trust me enough to share even her body. As I left her house I couldn't muster enough strength to look back. To avoid seeing anyone from the neighborhood, I took different streets to accept my crying and made my way back to my grands.

When I entered the house my cousin approached me and asked me to speak with him privately. When we entered his room, motioned for me to sit on my bed and then he stepped out of his room to look about for the presence of anyone. Then he came back in closed and locked the door. That's when he sat down to explain to me that he knew that our aunt played the game with me. I said yes but wanted to know how he knew. He looked at me and explained that our aunt told him and that when she was finished with me that he was next. He looked nervous telling me this and as always we had to plan our moves so that we were not left alone anywhere the rest of the night that would give her an opportunity to make us play. My cousin looked me over to see any visible signs of my distress. Then he asked me was I okay and I said no. He asked me was this act going to affect the relationship between my girlfriend and me. I said it already did. He sat back on his bed and paused. He then asked me did I tell her about our aunt's game. I explained no and that I didn't want to do it anymore. He said that she (our aunt) might tell her (my girlfriend) if I didn't. I said that she already told me that. He sat back again on his bed and asked me what we could do to stop it. I tried to think of something. My cousin also said that with two of us our aunt could have a field day. I assured him that I would not leave his side while I stayed. He thanked me but said it was hell trying to get away from her when I was away. I asked him to leave with me and we could stay at my house for the rest of the summer. He said he tried that once. Our aunt met him at a bus stop that our uncle dropped him off at and told him to go on home and prepare to play. I sat on the other bed and asked him for advice. He just lay back on his bed and the two of us laid there in silence.

This act with my aunt caused me a heavy burden to bear. I didn't know what my next plan to address her efforts was. I felt trapped and knew that there was a little time left before my girlfriend would find out. This part I was hoping she didn't find out but I knew we were going to have some real rocky times. To place more pressure on our relationship, my aunt continued to have her way with me with more frequency. She kept me busy with her so much that my girlfriend truly believed that I was cheating. My sometimes tired demeanor was a clear indication. We continued to maintain our relationship through my endeavors with my aunt and her accusations of infidelity until she grew tired.

I had a girl and lost a girl in a matter of months over my aunt's persistence. My girlfriend breaking up with me cut deep and I didn't have a explanation to hold her. I cried in my pillow until I went to sleep that day and on several other occasions. My cousin tried to comfort me the next morning but I had made up my mind while I slept that night. I told my cousin that I couldn't take it anymore and I wanted to leave early. My cousin understood why I said I had to go. He explained that he was okay with avoiding our aunt until she would become angry. My girlfriend was the tip of the ice berg where I had to make up my mind which route I was going to have to take when dealing with my aunt. I had just turned thirteen and I had had my first love and lost love all in the same summer.

My wife was surprised at my diligence to stay put and gazing about the crowd. As she approached me she could tell that I was in deep thought. She inquired and I said it was nothing, just memories from the past. My wife accepted the facts and asked me to help her find the kids. It took little time to find them with the other kids who were dragged into attending this gala. As we prepared to leave they explained how they enjoyed the night despite the adults passing by snooping on them as if they were going to spike the punch or sneak a alcoholic drink. They laughed, my wife smiled and I held the thought from earlier that night. At home I was a complete bore to my wife and she gave me space to breathe. We entered our bed with embrace until we fell asleep.

Benefaction

In my haste to meet up with my cousin after work, I didn't have time to freshen up. I had been outside most of the day working in hot weather without any air conditioning. So I decided to make a quick stop back at the office since I was still in the downtown vicinity, freshen up and change before meeting my cousin. It was a good thing that I always kept two clean shirts and a couple of ties handy for just such an emergency.

I didn't have to wait long at the hostess' desk; she was quite pleasant and allowed me through to enjoy myself of the festivities. I made my way through the crowd at the jazz club, looking about for my cousin who was nowhere in sight. The music and the ladies went hand in hand…"excuse me, pardon me, oh I sorry Miss…no um I'm trying to go this direction…" It wasn't until I stopped at the bar to order a nonalcoholic drink that I spotted my cousin in a booth with his girlfriend. For some reason he was looking in the other direction as if he was looking for me. As I weaved through the crowd to where he was sitting, it dawned on me to sneak up on him to give him a little scare. It didn't work because his girlfriend saw me, alerted him of my arrival and told him not to be alarmed when I approached. The two of them sat there trying to pretend to be oblivious to anything behind them. So I didn't try but instead pretended as if I'd stumbled and was about to spill my drink on his girlfriend. She screeched and tried to jump up and over his lap. That almost caused him to spill his drink and he looked at her awkwardly. I sat down immediately with my surprise.

We started to talk about why I didn't bring my wife and she would be mad if she found out. His girlfriend asked about my kids and to give her an update on my niece's adjustment with my family. We talked briefly about our sisters and I mentioned that I hadn't seen mine in weeks and that I was meaning to call them. My cousin called me a liar and said that he has spoken in depth with his sisters as well as mine. I brushed off his explanation and asked about my aunt, his mother. He reciprocated about mine but did mention that he spoke with both of them extensively. This too got me wondering so I inquired about his speaking with relatives in length and that's when he said that he and his girlfriend were now engaged. My mouth dropped and from other areas of the club came many of my cousin's fiancé's friends and family. I was introduced to her brothers and sisters, some cousins and good friends. She mentioned to me that her parents couldn't make it out on such short notice.

It was a complete surprise and he pulled me closer to whisper, "…by the way, your wife does know about this. Now the four us will have to go out later to celebrate and your wife is making the arrangements as we speak". I was totally taken by surprise and very happy for him and even more surprised when his fiancé asked me to be his best man instead of him. She said that my cousin had me on his mind the entire time after he proposed. I was speechless and then we started to enjoy the festivities. As people came and left congratulating my cousin's fiancé, he thought that now would be a good time to speak with me in detail somewhere private. So my cousin led me to one of the offices that belonged to one his friends who managed at the club.

We sat down at a table and chair set that was used for conferencing and poured two drinks from the small bar for our own celebration. I was still in a bit of a shock when my cousin explained that he wanted to jump right into what he wanted to talk with me. I prepared myself because I didn't know what to expect at this point. He started out about how he proposed to his fiancé and what steps he had taken to get to this point. I followed and then he spoke about our discussion that he didn't want to hear at the cookout and I followed that trying to conclude before he gave me the surprise. He followed up with his taking heed to what we talked about and how it got him to think about his own future. I demonstrated to him that I was following him by reciting what he said back to him in my own words. Then he said that he spoke in great detail about himself when he was younger to his fiancé and she convinced him to go and see a psychiatrist. I was waiting on his every word when he said that he had explained to his fiancé his trouble growing up. My mouth dropped on both statements and he waited for my response. At first I was terrified that someone else outside of our circle knew our secret and now this person would tell everyone, including my wife. My panic showed not only on my face but in my mannerism as I tried to stand, sit and fidget about the chair. My cousin reached across the table to assure me all was well but I jerked away from him and called him a betrayer. He chuckled at the thought and again asked me to calm down so that he could finish the rest of the story. But I couldn't control myself and stood up prancing about the office. I was trying to piece together my wife's reaction to her discovery and my responses. At this point I started to mumble to myself, trying to calm myself and then my cousin stood and called to me. I turned and looked at him and he explained in a calm voice that I should sit down.

I sat trying to keep my composure to what he would say next, but to my surprise he started to explain to me why he did what did. He said that he had been suppressing his feelings of betrayal, vindictiveness and disrespect since the first day of his encounter with our aunt. That was a lot for me to take in, but he went on to say that even though he was older in age he looked up to me and because of that admiration he thought about what I said. I kept on listening to him as if I was a child being feed to relieve hunger. My cousin poured out his heart about how much our aunt had took away a little of him each time.

I started to fight back the tears that were forming and the heartfelt release for him that he was being freed from his demons. I could see the joy across his face and how comfortable he felt talking about his journey to healing. I could see our positions being switched, the last time it was I who pushed, prodded him to face his demons and yet here and now it is he who is telling me! He moved around the table and sat in the chair next to me to plead with me to tell my wife about that part of my childhood she doesn't know about. Now I push away similar to how he did before and became reluctant to take heed to his pleading. So I stood, moved away from the table and pretended to prepare another drink when he moved with me and started in a different manner. My cousin asked me if I'd considered my children and the effects on them if they found out before my wife or at all. Again I was looking for a way, a method to close down my cousin's approach. I reached out and to my cousin it looked as if I was reaching out to him. In fact, I was reaching out to grab hold of something to support myself from falling. I didn't know how overwhelmed by this conversation. My cousin held me until I was able to plant my bottom in the chair I was sitting in before. He waited for me to make sense of my place and took the other chair to examine me. I tried to look away so that he couldn't get a clear idea if I needed a doctor. My cousin sat back in his chair and just waited for me to indicate that I was alright. It didn't take long for me to clear my head and I used this moment to fend off my cousin's persistence to seek help for a change. I held strong until our moment became useless and my cousin realized that we had been in this office too long. He checked his watch and explained that we should go. Bu t before we left, he told me that what we were talking about will be discussed later. He went further to say that his fiancé has moved past what he told her and now is looking for ways to help in his healing. I congratulated him again and he looked at me with a stare. I started to do the same when he backed away to recommend that I should tell my wife before she discovers it on her own.

Before we could walk to the end of the corridor his fiancé appeared and inquired if we would be joining the rest of the party. I explained to her that I wasn't going to be staying much longer because I hadn't been home since this morning. She looked at me with concern and asked me if I was doing alright. My cousin interrupted and explained that I'd had a long day and was starting to wind down. However, she wouldn't let up and tried to mention to me that what my cousin and she talked about was more about sharing about each other. She went on to say that their sharing will helped them both so that the other would know how and when related feeling to those past experiences would surface. I acknowledged what she was trying to say to me, but my mind was made up, she was the enemy. She knew too much and for that I would have to keep my distance as well as keep an eye on her when my woman is around her. Why did she have to be such a bitch when I liked by her family?

I finally bid her family and friends a goodbye and looked in my cousin's direction to give him a hint about what we talked about earlier. He looked at me with kindness and care, gave me a nod and waved. I started to turn when I could him my cousin saying that he would call me or that I should call him tomorrow. I waved again not turning around and left.

The drive home was a frustrating one where I keep talking with myself. I was so wired from my cousin's fiancé knowing of our depressing childhood that I began to feed my despair with directed despising of her. In turn I tried to curse my cousin for telling her. To me, we had sworn a pact, looked out for one another and tried to console one another in the beginning as well as later in life. We discovered how to avoid our aunt's attacks, remind one another that the other would always be supportive. Shared anything we had to keep the other's mind off of an incident. Helped cleaned one another after an episode and this is how he repays me? I now felt betrayed by him and entertained thoughts of how I could exact revenge on him. We endured this matter, not her. For he knows she could be out one day somewhere and start blabbering off to one of her friends. What a bitch! I should've cursed her out while I had the chance! But I'll see her again, and when I do I'll have something either on her or something for her. She'll know and feel what it's like to be a part of something so sacred and to betray that trust. But how could my brother do this to me for a trick? As I flung my hands, sometimes my arms and spoke in a loud tone, I didn't realize how my animation alerted people. Here I was at a traffic light going through my antics when someone behind me hit their horn. Startled I stopped and looked back to see who had done it. Unfortunately I wouldn't have found out but then realize that if it wasn't for the windows of my car being rolled up many people would've heard me. Besides the traffic light hadn't turn green yet and my actions were in full bloom. I tried to calm down as some of the other drivers that had an opportunity to pass me gave me looks of concern as if I was crazy or something. The embarrassment I should've felt at that moment wasn't there and I crossed the next intersection before the light turned yellow.

For some reason I was exhausted from the drive home. I was hunger tired and my head was finally coming to rest instead of all that spinning earlier in the evening. My entry into my house didn't alert anyone because I paused to listen for nay movements or sounds. Nothing. I moved through the living room and figured I try to get something from the refrigerator when I saw a dim light from the basement. I figured someone left a light on and forgot to turn it off. For the moment I would ignore the light and rummage through the refrigerator until I found something that would match my hunger. I sat there in dim lights at the kitchen table eating my tuna salad sandwich trying to piece together the events past between my cousin and I.

I recall the events after my first encounter. My cousin woke my playing with my ears until I told him to quit it. He whispered to me that our favorite show was about to come on and we needed to get downstairs before our sisters did. That way we could commandeer the TV set for a couple of shows. I sat up and looked about our room for something to put on. He was already somewhere in the middle of the staircase waving me on to hurry up. Instead of getting dressed, I just carried my clothes with me. Downstairs during a commercial he inquired about my being up stairs so long last night. I brushed off any notion he had of my being mischievous. But he pursued me with more questions until I told him to promise not to tell. Right then and there he thought that the moment I'd experienced would never happen again. But when it did, I could see sadness and helplessness in his eyes and he tried to stay with me to prevent the incident from happening again.

I couldn't eat anymore and felt as though I needed to eat some more but I just couldn't. I wrapped up the rest of my sandwich, drank my juice and started toward the dining room when I decided to venture to the light. I opened the door and descended the basement steps. I could see more of the light and now recognized that someone had left the computer on. But there were other silhouettes of color blending in with this light as I got closer. So I walked on a little now concerned about the computer being left on. Then I noticed a figure behind the screen. I didn't want to alarm the person but was curious as to why they were down in the basement with the computer on in the dark. The closer I got the less they were concerned with my approach. So as I moved pass the table that held the computer…

I was like seeing a mirror image of myself. He was just building himself up gazing at the images with a crazed look of addiction. When he looked up he fell off the chair and scrambled to cover himself up. I just stood there in amazement. He kept apologizing for what was on the screen stating that he found it on the system when he started it up. Again I couldn't move because of what I was seeing and felt sad for my boy. I took him a little time to position himself in his clothes and fix himself appropriately. I tried to talk but nothing came out as I thought of myself and my last conversation with my cousin. Believe it or not my son started to walk away saying he would be back in few but first he had to go use the bathroom. As calmly as I could, I called him back to me and invited him to sit back down at the computer table. He came back slowly looking as if he was trying to come up with more ways of denial. I had to remove my hand from my mouth in order to start our dialogue. I started out with how he knew about the computer being downstairs. He looked at me as if I was setting him up before I chastise him. I assured him there would be no beatings what so ever regarding this matter. He had forgotten just that fast about my question. It took him a moment to refocus his thoughts and explained that he had caught his sisters and his cousin down here one night whispering about something that was on the computer. I asked him how long had this been going on. He tried to leave out details and explained that he caught his sisters either earlier this year or late last year talking about this computer in the basement. I again started to feel light headed and tried to control the saying in my head. I asked him who left the computer on so that the girls could see this stuff. He said it was me and that he and his sisters knew how to find the imbedded sites last visited even if you delete the past history. I could've been proud of him and sisters for their prowess to master computer surfing, but we needed to talk in more detail. I could tell that he wanted to give only a portion of how all of this came about and I pressed him for more information. He tried to build the sorrow and shame in his voice and started to tremble a little. I couldn't let up and moved closer to him to make him aware of how serious this matter was that we were dealing with at this moment. I waited a few moments in order to collect myself and then I asked him how did he know about the web and such. He paused and I said that we were too deep into this matter for him not to come clean with what he knew. My boy, my son, bowed his head and eventually started to shake it in a defiant last stand. I told him to look up at me, and he kept shaking his head in a defiant no. I reached to grab him about his shoulders, he looked up at me at the same instant, mouth gapped open in preparation for some chastisement and said, "…from you!!!"

We sat there with his constant wiping of his tears on his shirt sleeves, in his hands and then onto his pants. I started to hang my head because I couldn't' believe so much could happen in such a short time frame. I asked my son in a soft voice reflecting on my own experiences with my cousin of when did this start for him. He sniffed and shock nervously at times but manage to muster up enough strength to start talking. He started with when we had gotten our second computer and I was spending so much time on the computer. Well when his sisters were on one he asked his mother could he use the other one and she said yes. But before he could navigate he ran into some trouble and asked his sisters to help him. That's when his oldest sister discovered the links and sort, but she never told him that they were embedded on the computer. So as time passed he didn't give it any thought about why his sisters always wanted to use the other computer, the one he started on. It wasn't until one day that his mother wanted to use the one he was on for a few minutes. That caused him to join his sisters and that's when he discovered the sites because they were looking through them. But because it was he and he is a male his sisters didn't want to look anymore while he was there. But for some reason, his sisters stopped using that computer, maybe because they felt awkward looking at the computer images with someone of the opposite sex, especially their brother. So after that moment with his sisters, he was back to the other computer using it by himself. Now my daughters are involved with my mess too. My son goes on with hearing some of his friends talking in school about different sites and he joined in one day telling them of some of the ones he'd found. With that information and with the ones his friends already knew about, that group began more in depth searching and here we are now.

    My son started to cry with shame and started to cover his face. At this moment I had an opportunity to connect with by admitting some of my wrong doing which helped to lead to this moment, but instead I held back that part about me. Instead I consoled him and explain that he had to start keeping this matter of his under control or else if anyone else finds out then he'd have to see me. He looked at me as if I was crazy. He couldn't believe that he could get off that easy from such a matter when he was "thrown under a bridge" (not literally) for smaller infractions of conduct. Before he could questioned me why such a light scolding, I explained to him that there are mistakes we all make in life. I continued with mistakes have to be learned form or else there is no change and I asked him how did he feel being caught. He explained scared, embarrassed and fearful of what was going to done with the incident, like telling his mom or his sisters or better yet his friends. I asked him what if I told his friends and his mother because his sisters already have some idea. He couldn't answer because he kept playing different scenarios in his mind. Our hypothesizing of this matter worked and that is what I was getting across to him.

    He felt relieved but still shaken and he tried to thank me for not "killing" (not literally) him. I laughed at his remorse and explained to him that if this ever came up again that he would have to deal with me first and he acknowledged the consequences. I told him to head on upstairs to finish cleaning up and that I'd clean up the computer. As he stopped at the bottom of the stairs, he turned to ask me a question. I took my time to look in his direction to let him know that I was now becoming annoyed with our talk. But he waited and with his opportunity he wasted no time in turning the tables back on me. He asked me why I loaded the links on the computer, why did I do it in the first place and lastly did I ever do what he just did when I caught him. I wanted to answer him quickly before my hesitation would give me away. I answered him by explaining that like his friends my friends would send me links and I'd hear about this and about that but I only perused through them to see what the interest was about. Furthermore I continued that I've never had an inkling or notion to do what he did but I had heard of people and some of my friends doing that for more than one reason. He contemplated my answers and replied with asking me if what he was doing made him a sickly person. Oh God, again I couldn't tell him how we were more linked that what he could fathom. So I told him that when you don't know if something is right or wrong before you do it, it's best to ask someone of adult age if they can explain to you about the wrong and right of the matter. He interrupted me and explained that telling someone something like that isn't something you can just talk about to anyone. I told him he was correct and that's why I'm around.

Manifestation

You can tell when the summer season is coming to a close, the weather changes a bit, the sun seems to hang a little lower and light winds come from any and everywhere. You tend to see some of the people you haven't seen in a while and the attitudes of the children change. For the latter allow me to explain, the kids in my house started to discuss the latest clothing styles, the new trendy sayings, who was going to what classes and last, the preparation for my niece to leave. Her imminent departure was nearing and everyone was sensing it. There could be no comforting words or alterations for what was to happen, the realization of her being a family visitor was something we could not change. She has transcended that initial thought after being here so long and of course enduring our ever changing behavior.

As always, things around the house looked bright for this particular day but I could sense that there was something different in the air. My pessimistic attitude did not help to quench this mood and to make matters worse I sought to construct this attitude of mine a priority. I moved about the house with an alertness that would signal the initial characteristic of the mood. That approach actually held everyone else in the house in a relatively similar mood. As I would interact with each member, I could see a slight change in how they observed me. However, in that encounter, neither of us would speak of our acknowledgement.

I walked past my girls' room and decided to open up the half closed door. Forgetting to knock, as I entered, they weren't even surprised by my sudden presence. They just continued on with what they were doing and basically ignored me. I approached them between their beds and tried to engage them in conversation. They played along by entertaining me with respect, but my oldest tried desperately not to make eye contact with me. At first I wanted to inquire about her actions, and I thought they must be talking "girl" talk which doesn't require a male. I announce my departure and they tried to be nonchalant about my leaving as not draw my attention back to them again. So as I left, I peered back to see if they would react differently, nothing. Either they had figured me out or they were truly involved in something that I could not relate.

My wife yelled from her room for my presence. I confirmed her loud voice with a response and informed her I was en route. As I passed the bathroom which connected both the rooms to my girls and my son, I noticed movement in the form of a shadow coming from the bathroom. I paused then proceeded to attend to my wife at the other end of the long hallway. As I grabbed the door to my bedroom, I glanced back to see my niece leaving the once open and unlit bathroom. At this point I was wavering as to which to give my attention; my wife, who called for me by name, or my niece, because there was more to her movement than what I saw. I decided to visit that scene later and attend to my wife.

Inside as I lay across the foot of our bed, my wife sat with her back to the headboard with bent legs. She was reading some type of book with a blank hardback cover and rubbing her feet back and forth. I took this as a hint and moved closer when she peered from over her book and asked me how I felt about our niece's scheduled departure. I tried to explain the loss I would feel and how her presence was a breath of fresh air. My wife listened intently and proposed that because our niece was the youngest in her family and that she wasn't a burden, why couldn't we see if she could stay and attend school in our neighborhood? I was surprised that my wife would insinuate such a proposal. I didn't want her to see my reluctance in having our niece around all the time. I wanted to deal with this matter with a very delicate dialect.

On the other hand, my prison was hinting that this would be the opportunity of a lifetime! My prison led me to intuitively see how easy infecting her would be for me. The methodical way I could approach her over time wouldn't take as long as I would think. I quickly imagined the many encounters where we would be left alone or better yet left in my care. Besides, she would be here, every day to face me whether she wanted to or not. As I embraced this form of yearning, reality struck me up side my head. I began to see the pain I could inflict, the constant attempts to justify mistrust directed toward her and my own thoughtlessness to allow the disbelief to take place. Once again I felt strange, almost filthy as I had the opportunity to have a glimpse of the repercussions.

My wife held the top of my head to pull me away from my stupor. When I came to, she just laughed at me and explained that she was only looking at me for about a minute but my facial expression showed intense thought. I brushed off her notion and told her I was thinking about the shorts she was wearing and how my mind started to wander. We explored the idea of our niece staying, trying to anticipate what her parents would say and how they would feel about the idea. We talked for quite some time until my wife realized that there was something she wanted to prepare for dinner tonight. I tried to convince her that she didn't have to tonight, but her mind was made up and she stepped over me before exiting our room.

I laid there across my bed for a minute thinking about all that my wife and I had just discussed and my apprehension of having my niece stay despite the idea being a good one. For a moment I didn't know what to do with myself and lightly entertained the thought of releasing my prison while my wife was downstairs. It was a good notion but the thought led me to back to what I experienced before I entered my room; that shadow and my niece leaving the bathroom after I walked past. So I forced myself up off the bed and moved toward my bedroom door. I paused and listened for any sounds so that I could spring something on one of the kids. Nothing. So as I opened my door, I noticed that the hallway was darker than it was before because all the lights from the other open rooms were turned off. I surmised that everyone was either downstairs or out. As I proceeded to walk down the hallway and couldn't shake a feeling that was coming over me. It felt weird and I couldn't place it but as I walked further I began to think about this girl who lived down the street from my old house.

She was friendly, cheerful and a friend of my sisters. Her overly-friendly attitude attracted me to her but for some reason I knew that I wasn't supposed to lay a hand on this girl. Some young adult intuitiveness held me in check from approaching her in any manner but only as her girlfriend's brother. This role I accepted because at the very least, I could still gaze upon her lustfully when she visited.

But she was a "touchy-feely" kind of person and I couldn't handle someone in my personal space for only that kind of interaction. What made it worst was this girl would come by and stay long periods of time and often stay overnight with my sisters and over time, to me, she became a household figure.

I had gotten so use to her being around I had forgotten about how I tried to look at her. I didn't want the numbing that felt I endured with my prison when she was in my presence. Oftentimes when she would visit, I tried to encourage my prison to come forth so that I could give her a small taste of the power it held over me. At this point, my prison was my curse and I was still wrestling with the power it could hold for me. So this part of me didn't hinder my attraction to her, but I couldn't get past the feeling that something would keep us apart no matter how I tried.

But this girl would tempt fate between us and thus ruin any type of relationship that we would have, even at a distant. Once after school as part of my usual routine, I would come home and nap for awhile, later get up to complete my homework and then eat dinner. This routine was like clockwork; methodical. However, this day would change the way we looked at each other. I was asleep with my door cracked open and in a distant, I could hear my sister and a few girls talking as they approached the front door of our house. They talked about this or that, I couldn't make out the words but I just kept hearing voices. The group finally made their way up stairs to congregate in my sisters' room. I could hear the constant talking and then the stereo playing some love songs for which they sang along. This gathering went on for quite some time but I'm not sure because I had grown use to the noise and had fallen back into a deep sleep.

As I started to awake again I could hear my sisters talking with one of her girlfriends instead of many. It was peculiar but I tried once again to ignore their talking. For some odd reason as my sister and her girlfriend were walking past my room they decided to enter and see what I was doing. They noticed that I had my back to them because I would sleep facing the wall. So in order to provoke a reaction out of me, this same friendly girl sat on my bed and continued to speak with one of my sisters who sat at my desk. I tried to ignore them but they continued to talk about this or that and eventually they got a little rise out of me. However, I spoke from my position of facing the wall. I announced to them who the room belong to and inquired why they were in my room. They both giggled and the friendly girl explained that she was curious as to why every day I would take a nap in the late afternoon after school. I tried to explain my rising up early and sports and having a lunch period so close to school ending for the day. As I spoke the two of them continued on another subject and I gave up trying. Because of my ignoring them they eventually left and didn't return.

However as days would past and my sisters' routine with her girlfriends become evident, now and then the girlfriend would come in my room walk about touching things and ask me questions. So to address that behavior with offending I started to close my door. This effort did not stop my sister and the girlfriend. The two of them would enter my room without knocking and once again the girlfriend would sit on my bed next to me. She became so accustomed to doing this that one day she laid on my bed next to and pretended to fall asleep. My sisters were amused at this and tried the same thing. My tolerance for sharing a bed became too much and I arose and left the two of them in my room. When I returned they had left and I found my place to snuggle up against the wall.

Finally after a few more playful interactions, this girlfriend decided to come in my room without my sister and lay in my bed next to me. This particular day I was tired and at this point I didn't care as long as she didn't touch me. Over time I could hear the voices of my sisters and their friends but they were faint. As I began to awake I listened for one of my sisters and their friends, I heard nothing. But I could feel a presence next to me. It was the girlfriend and she too was awakening. I paused to check for the presence of my sister and was astonished that she was not in the house. I looked back to the girlfriend and she look over at me with such an alluring smile that I felt a rise from my prison. So in order to bring out my prison I had to first let her know how much I was interested in her. As I touched the girlfriend around her waist she let out a long drawn breath and I proceeded to advance myself. I turned her over and kissed her along her neck. The girlfriend moved her arms up above her head and rested them on the pillow she laid her head. I started to feel across her chest and she finally moved a hand gently over my head. I was amassed and moved at the same time of her response. So I started to move over and on top her. The girlfriend didn't refuse my advances and I moved her legs open by pushing hers with mine. The other hand of the girlfriend's laid just under my shoulder I my prison was in full swing. My manhood rose and I pressed against her so that she could feel the presence. I moved my head up to kiss her and she looked at me with trusting and assured eyes. Oh I dreamt once or twice about a moment like this with her and now I was going to have one. I kissed her gently as to not alarm her and started to use my tongue. Again she didn't refuse and started to become more involved in the act. I tried my best not to be aggressive so that I wouldn't scare her, but her smell, her touch, her taste was overwhelming. We continued for a little longer and then I decided to take our venture to the next stage. I was hoping she would not refuse me advances. I pushed up from her and moved one of my hands to unzip her jeans waiting for her to respond negatively. She didn't and I proceeded with unzipping my jeans. Again she did not move to the contrary and I started to slide her jeans down, a side at a time. I was excited and nervous at the same time and I had gotten her jeans down past her knees. My arms became weary but I held on to reach down and slide the girlfriend's panties down from her rear. She looked at me curiously and waited patiently for my next move. I pushed myself off of her and started to work her panties down a little farther. That's when she started to whisper something to me, but she wasn't looking in my direction. At first I thought she was in another world and speaking out in relation to the moment. As I continued the girlfriend turned to slowly look in my direction, softly asked me to stop and started to apologize about the whole thing. I tried to ignore her because I wanted to see at least what she looked like between her legs. She quickly grabbed my arm and started to calmly plead with me. I whispered to her that we weren't going any further but I wanted to see her if that was okay. The girlfriend sprang up and I reacted with my arm snapping away her as if I was reacting to being burnt. She stood and tried to quickly dress, I slid to the side of the bed and tried to do the same. Fortunately, I was able to dress before her and stepped between her and my bedroom door. She looked at me and began to plead with me in a mild rising panic. I stood motionless admiring the effects of the moment because I was becoming frustrated with how this episode was going. The girlfriend began prostrating herself in a begging manner, her arms moving in a rigid but frantic motion. Again the girlfriend continued apologizing for her initial actions hoping for her release. I could see she was on the brink of crying and because I was disappointed, I waited to see her cry. As she waited for my response, I didn't budge and I could see in her a realization that she might have to go through with my wishes before she would be allowed to leave my room. In a last attempt she rushed toward me, trying to throw me off balance in order to obtain her release. This didn't work because I anticipated this move and braced myself. Also she was not very strong in her upper body and I just grabbed her arms and placed her off balanced. The girlfriend stumbled and then she tried to scream in desperation. I bent down and moved to place a hand over her mouth. In my kneeling position, she tried to reach up and scratch me about my face. I was able to grab one of her arms but she left a bruise across my neck. It stung because I felt the ripping of my flesh. It didn't matter at this point because I wasn't disappointed anymore but now mad. I was enraged because she started this and now after playing games she wanted to end this matter, the tease. In my now madden state of mind, I lifted her up to her feet and began to twist the arm I held. The girlfriend started to lean over trying to endure the twisting of her arm. By doing this I was able to position myself behind her. She tried to look over her shoulder but I twisted her arm a little tighter each time. For a moment I just her there hoping she would concede to my earlier wish. But instead with all her might, she was able to kick back one of her legs and catch me briefly between my legs. I felt the pain slowly rise up into my gut and my legs starting to weaken. The act made me feel queasy and nauseous. As my leg began to buckle, the girlfriend noticed my grip on her arm lessening and she began trying to free herself. At first I couldn't hold her, covered my groin area with my free hand to alleviate some of the pain and held myself up under buckling knees, but I managed. However, she was able to break free from the twist but I held her arm and she made her way to my bedroom door. The girlfriend turned and with her free hand, she began swinging in my direction and hitting me on occasion. I ducked and dodged some punches, attempts at scratching and absorbed several but I held on to her arm. She basically drugged me toward the bedroom door where she able to grab hold of the doorknob. I had gotten some of my strength back by now and tried to stand erect in order to balance myself. After doing so I tightened my grip again on her arm and tried to apply twist to her arm. However, she was working frantically at this moment and was able to open the door. She pulled on it until it opened completely and then began to yell. I couldn't hold her mouth and instead tried to apply my twist again. It had become apparent to me that at this point it didn't matter how much twisting I applied, she was halfway free and nothing was going to stop her. The girlfriend realize that the only people in my house was her I and she ceased her screaming. She quickly turned to look at me and explain that I should stop, that this intense moment was going nowhere fast and that if I let her go now she would not tell what happened. The telling part was something I almost forgot and slowly began to release my grip on her. I was hoping my gesture would persuade her not to tell. She stood there in the doorway between my room and the long hallway, looking down the hall to make certain of her getaway if necessary. It looked to me as if she was trying to focus on the surroundings of the hallway because it was now evening and there were no other lights on but the one from my room. My room cast a long bright beam of light which lightened up everything that crossed its path. It looked as if it didn't filter into the edges of the darkness. I waited for a reaction as she began to gather her faculties in order to explain something to me. The girlfriend went on to explain that this entire fiasco was not her intention nor was it all her fault. I countered with she should be apologizing to me because she came into my room. We paused with nothing to say to one another and that's when she started to leave. I grabbed her again by her arm to be assured that she wouldn't tell anyone. She looked at her clothes, the bruises on her arm and began to explain that she was going to leave. I didn't move. As she started down the steps I moved to the top of the staircase to watch her leave.

     The girlfriend never looked back, but I could tell she was nervous about not leaving. She eased into each step as if to not make a sound. Out of frustration, I rushed down the stairs to stop her, I don't know why I tried this action, but the girlfriend started to run to the door. I was able to bridge her action of getting to the door before me and this caused her to stumble toward the door. As I approached her, she started to plead with me for her release. For a moment she explained that she would do almost anything if I would just let her leave. I was intrigued by her panic but I wanted her to suffer a little more for tempting my prison to release. As she started to cry, I felt pity, turned to make a path for her to leave and looked away from her. She started on her journey to the front door with apprehension and as she nervously got the door the open, she looked back to me, yelled a few epithets at me and ran down the steps away from my house. The girlfriend stumbled a bit and once she reached the sidewalk, she noticed another girl who was walking by look at her with curiosity when they met. The girlfriend tried to maintain her composure as she and the girl walked and talked. I stood at the front door looking onward and caught the eye of the other girl looking back at me as the girlfriend continued talking. I prayed within myself that because the other girl noticed this girlfriend leaving my house that this act would pose doubt as to what really happened. In the weeks, months that followed the girlfriend never stayed long or didn't visit at all to my house. Not even my sisters noticed the change in her behavior. In addition, when our paths crossed, the girlfriend became nervous and fidgeted when she stayed too long. The girlfriend never held a conversation with me from that point forward.

Later in my life before I became involved with my wife, I fabricated a story around these same circumstances to a few older friends in conversation at a gathering. Many of them explained to me in detail that what I was explaining was a definite case of rape. Even though I fabricated the story it left an impression on them that regardless of my age at the time, the girlfriend could've brought charges against me. After knowing that what I'd done was something of extraordinary circumstances, I left the party for home. There I searched for a place in my bedroom to cry myself almost every night before going to sleep. I carried that shame for at least well over a half of a year, never telling anyone and trying to behave normal.

Since that time I have seen the girlfriend from time to time when I was in my old neighborhood. The last time I saw her I tried to approach her to apologize and again ask for forgiveness, but our encounter was short lived. Then again I'm not sure if I could face her again and that is why I allowed the moment to past between us. I'm not sure if she's married, but she seems to be functioning as an adult pretty well, from what I saw of her from afar. On occasion I've given thought about our incident, justifying it with being young with no real understanding. Yet it is something that I know will someday again surface for my judgment has not been fulfilled.

As I walked my hallway to descend the staircase the thoughts of this incident still loomed greatly over me. My mind was playing segments in slow motion as I moved about. In my movement, as I now looked over my stairs as I stepped, my living room as I walked, then into my dining room, I could not shake the thoughts and feelings that overcame me related to the incident with the girlfriend. I even turned around to picture myself descending the staircase running after the girlfriend. What saved me from my own continued punishment was the noise I heard from the other side of the front door. The noise was of a group and evolving as it seemed to approach my house. The voices were now distinguishable enough for me to recognize that it was the voices from my kids. It also alerted me that my kids were on their way inside the house.

Appetition

My wife fidgeted at the computer trying to keep her focus. She has been at the computer playing what I call her time for "school". You see she has been looking over a budget she made for the kids for the upcoming school year. What makes this budget a little different is that it now includes our niece. So I sit next to her at the table in the small enclave off the kitchen to offer my support. We have been looking over some extra-curriculum items where we can make adjustments for accommodating our niece. Apparently her parents finally conceded to allowing her to stay for the upcoming school year. But they have given us certain requirements in order to form this deal. Thus far we have taken all the necessary steps to making this venture happen. One deal that my wife's cousin made was that she would like to see more of her daughter while she stayed with us as. Another was that we had to provide everything including half the clothing bill. In the meantime we hadn't finished the school transfer paperwork because the legality of this move meant we had to present the illusion to the school that we had full custody of our niece. The frustrating part of this matter is that my wife hasn't been able to find any other addendums to her budget. So I offer her a chance to break away for a moment by sitting in our lounge chair in the living room. She finally gets up and moved to the living room and I follow.

As we lay around in the living room listening to some music, I can hear our youngest daughter making her way downstairs and into the kitchen. We don't give in to her movements nor do we even give into checking on her movements. However, after my wife has begun to relax and think of other ways she has not explored on our budget, I realize that our youngest has not left the kitchen. So I go to check on her and I guess she heard me before I could hear her next move. When I enter the kitchen my youngest tries not to look surprise but I can tell she is up to something, I just can't tell what it is. I try to question her but she avoids answering me by preoccupying herself with looking for something in the cabinets. I try once more but she doesn't want me to know what the problem is. I don't press her because she has such a concerned looked about her face and I wonder if it's boy trouble. So I ask her if that is the problem and she answers me with disgusted "no". By the way she answers me and the look on her face I know it's not that. This alarms my wife because I believe we've elevated our voices in our conversation and she enters the kitchen with a motherly approach to our daughter. She lures our daughter over to the refrigerator and starts to whispers with her. From my vantage point all I can hear is my daughter nodding and my wife occasionally looking over her shoulder to determine my whereabouts. It looks as if my wife can pry out the true answer to what ails our youngest, but I can't tell. So as to not derail their conversation I make my way back to the living room.

 I can hear my wife and my daughter conversing in such a low tone that it sounds like mumbling. To get a better chance at listening I sit up and lean slightly over the back of the couch so that their voices can carry over my head. That's when I catch some shadow movement out the corner of my eye from the stairs. I wait to convince myself if what I saw was what I saw. But the curiosity gets the best of me and I move to ascend the steps to the upstairs. However my movement has alarmed the shadow figure. I rush upstairs but when I reach the landing it's as if there was never anyone there. I stand in place and listen for sounds. Nothing. Discouraged, I start for my bedroom and as I pass the hallway bathroom I hesitate because I recall what happened the last time. All I want to do is catch the person; I'm not sure what I'd do next if I caught them. To me the culprit has to be up to something deceptive. So I peek into the bathroom door that is ajar and again nothing. But as I start back to open my bedroom door I sense movement from the bathroom again and as I look over my shoulder I thought I saw my niece leaving the bathroom. So to prove to myself once and for all that what I heard and thought I saw was true I head to the bathroom. There I catch my son leaving, but with the light off. I stop him to inquire.

 At first his explanation was he just didn't turn on the light while in the bathroom. But I pressed him as he tried to move about his room in an awkward manner. That movement indicated to me that something else was going on with him. He continued to move about his room slowly and instead of physically following him, I took a seat at his desk and admired his uneasiness.

That's when I asked him to turn around. He acted as if he didn't hear me. I asked again with more forcefulness. Again he didn't want to respond. So as I started to stand, he slowly turned only allowing me to see most of his body from the side. That's when I noticed what was left of his boyhood pressed heavily up against his shorts. I felt more embarrassed for him than he felt embarrassed about being seen. He still tried to lean over some as to not give away more protrusion. I asked him what he was doing to cause him to physically show up in that manner. He didn't want to answer me. I pressed him for the "why". He said it was nothing and that he was just excited. I countered with that there is only one way why a male becomes excited like he is right now, so I pressed him for more information. He fidgeted with his clothes and started to twitched nervously. I reached to grab his arm and he withdrew himself in a scared excitement. I stopped in my motion a little astonished by his reaction and explained to him that he was either going to tell me why he ended up in that state or we was going to be here for as long as it took. My son tried to take me up on my offer but then he started to change his mind after we sat in silence for a moment. That was because he knew that I could cause him more inconvenience as we waited. He begged me not pressed him for more information, yet I continued to ignore his request. I didn't want him to feel so awkward but because of our standoff he started to tear. I tried to reassure him that this matter was going to be alright, that this was a continuation from our last encounter. I went on to tell him that depending on the circumstances, we could get through this one the same way. He started to cry softly and then he turned his back toward me to wipe his tears. I didn't move to comfort him and started to speak to him in a calm voice.

He tried to explain that it was all a big mistake and that nothing happened. I tried to slow him down in his rant but he continued on. My son, my boy, tried to assure me that it started before the pool party. He continued with it started out as a game and while they wrestled he inadvertently touched her and she basically ignored his touches. I tried to stop him to find out who was the girl. He started to beg me not to chastise him for what happened. I stood up to calm him down to figure out first who was the girl and what happened. My son, my son, in his infinite wisdom panicked and tried to run out of his room. I'm not sure if the embarrassment was too much for him that he knew he had to hide whatever the truth was from me. I grabbed him by his arm before he could get to the door and he shrieked as if he was already hit. I looked at him puzzled and again tried to calm him down. His voice rose as fast as he was trying to move. I became angry and asserted myself of my demands to my son. My son's voice became so loud that my wife and youngest daughter stormed into my son's room to find out what was the matter. I looked up at the two of them trying to assure my wife that what was happening was not what she thought. My youngest screamed in terror and my wife yelled at me for what she thought I was suspected of doing to my son. I tried to plead my innocence and my youngest kept screaming. At that point my wife quieted her and again began questioning me! I could not believe what was happening as my grip on my son's arm was weakening.

My wife, unsettled in her emotions wedged herself between our son and me. I looked down at her as if she was crazy. She looked up at me and insisted that I let go of her son. I was awe struck at her behavior and tried to now assure her that this matter could be resolved. In the ensuing conversation, my son started his rant of how I barged in his room with accusations. My wife looked at me with pity and I looked at my son who was still trying to get out of my grip. That's when I saw my eldest daughter and my niece looking on with curiosity.

I loosened my grip on my son, stood erect and looked about at everyone. For a split second it appeared to me as if I'd lost all control over my household and that notion angered me. I didn't want anyone to know this especially my wife so I paused before I spoke my words and kept my focus on all of them as much as I could. I was calming myself down and tried to explain to my wife that our son needed to be questioned about his behavior which was predicated on a meeting we had had earlier. My wife couldn't believe that what my son and I were doing was from something that was not settled earlier. By now my son has joined his sisters and it seemed that they were rallying around him. He stood in front of them but I could see them encircling him. My wife looked over the scene, realized that there was more to what she was seeing and considered the matter. After a few minutes of pure silence from everyone, my wife tuned toward me. She stood up on her toes and whispered to me that a scene like this was not something we'd condone as parents and that she only came up because she heard our son's screams as if I was trying to do him bodily harm. I wanted to laugh at her but I whispered back to her that we needed to talk privately about this matter. My wife turned to look in our son's direction and asked him if he wanted to tell her something before she and I went somewhere to discuss his behavior. My son stood firm hoping that I wouldn't tell his mom. He looked across toward me with a pleading face and I returned a look that would indicate that this matter was over and that I would tell. At this moment I knew he was what some call "feeling himself" and I that he didn't have a chance. But I allowed this matter to squelch because I had to decide how to not tell on my son but alert my wife that our son had some unresolved issues.

In our room my wife talked about the matter in a chronological fashion, breaking down details as I basically stood in front of her lying about what really happened between our son and me. She went on and on making the matter I was lying seem childish, insignificant and somewhat unrelated to the previous incident. I stood firm with my telling her that he was in some of my personal things that only she was allowed to explore. I continued with by our son being exposed to such things he could now surmise that he is on some level of understanding with us now. It seemed believable to me but it took awhile for my wife to ingest it.

It had become quiet in the house and you could hear murmurs coming from my daughters' room. It was apparent that everyone was meeting there to discuss the events and come to some conclusion. I knew that I was the bad guy in their eyes with my son painting the most bizarre picture of me as a father and uncle.

The adrenalin rush I experienced during the confrontation was something I hadn't felt since my last workout at the gym and I embraced it as usual. This allowed my prison to raise its ugly head and as usual it tapped me on my shoulder. I tried to disregard it but it slowly appealed to me, building me up with hypothetically. I started to give some of them some thought by then I wanted my wife to quench its thirst. But after our discussion I knew that she wouldn't be so receptive to the thought. So I conjured up a scheme to entertain my prison. I hadn't planned on how was the best approach to satisfying it but I pursued the opportunity. As soon as I gave it deeper thought I realized that the house was full. The only thing in my favor at the moment was that it was late evening. I was hoping that everyone would stay put and that I could go and entertain my prison, but the thought was now becoming a bore. I stopped in my living to question myself why was this change occurring within me. I disregarded it for the time being, I laid on the living room couch and started to channel surf.

The female was pleading with the male, asking him to stay. She was practically draped over him and he was trying to gently hold her hands away from his face. He knew something was coming but his anticipation didn't alert him to what it was. The female, distraught and overwhelmed with dejection, slumped her body over the male and started to slide down his body toward the floor. The male grabs her wrists and tries to brace her from falling. The female builds up her feeling of dejection and cries in a whimper, wiping her face on the male's shirt. The male looks down trying to soothe the female, assuring her that their relationship will endure this moment. But as the two embrace the female ponders their relationship and decides that if it is to end then it will end on her terms. The male unaware of this notion continues with his consoling until the female looks up into the face of the male and he returns a look of comfort to the female. She slowly pushes away and the male assists her by bracing her and pushing her up to stand on her own. The male has released his hold on her wrists and prepares for the unexpected. He looks at her and with a sad, grief stricken face; she knees him hard in his groin. The male bends over with a groan and attempts to cover himself. That's when the female lunges at him and begins to claw at his face.

It was similar to what she did to me that day I went to my grands to pick up my cousin so that we could go to this party downtown. We were of somewhat responsible age and our aunt was growing angry over our ability to not only avoid her but to stand firm against her quest to blackmail us with telling what we did together. I was looking for my cousin who had been delayed at the cleaners getting his shirt pressed. I tried not to hang around the house when she tried to sneak up on me. I made salutations with my aunt and she asked me if I'd seen any other family members. My response was that my grandfather was in the back of the house, my grandmother was out and that I hadn't seen anyone else since I'd been here. I wanted to give her all information so that she wouldn't ask me anything else. Instead she went after me right away and pleaded with me to come upstairs for quick game of let's play. I'd refused and she started to tug on my arm. I asked her to stop and thought I'd heard my grandfather doing something in the back and looked back at my aunt a little scared. I just didn't like any confrontations with her because it always seemed she was the victim. So she pressed me and then sat next to me to beg so more. I had flashbacks of one of our times when she had messed things up with my girlfriend and just didn't want to go through with it. My aunt move to straddle me and that's when I stood up but she fell before I could catch her. She grabbed her arm in pain and looked at me as if I'd struck her in retaliation. Her eyes filled with pain and she tried not to cry. I reached down in disgust to comfort her. She whimpered and explained that she needed me to do this for her because I was the only that could give her relief, not my cousin, me. I tried to tell her that I just couldn't anymore, I was older, she could be become pregnant and it was just wrong. She reached up and grabbed me around my neck to lift her up. I tried to brace myself as I helped her to her feet. She seemed to be limper as if the pain had not only intensified in her arm but her entire body. I was careful not to place any pressure on her damaged arm as started to lift her. My aunt finally made it to her feet and looked about herself to check for other problems. She looked up at me and told me how tall I had gotten. I was a bit embarrassed that she even knew that about me. We stood facing each other not touching. I started to tell her that what we had, it had to stop because it wasn't right and besides I was still having problems dealing with what we were doing. She looked down and away from me a little dejected by my explanation and said she would be okay with it for now. Relieved at her acknowledgement I reached over to give her a hug and that's when she kneed me (it felt like it was twice) in the groin. I felt excruciating pain, my eyes rolled in my head and I fell like a log. I knew I'd struck my head because later my cousin would tell me that he saw a purplish colored knot across my lower left jaw. The only thing that I could remember after my aunt tried to claw at my face was two things, my grandfather yelling at her, pulling her off of me, and her whispering in my ear before my grandfather could pull her off me. She said that I could never heal from what she gave me, that she had the power to give me the release I needed, and that she will forever be a part of my life, even if I never saw her again. I filled instantly with anger, but as I stood to apply some sort of physical damage to her. Our grands stepped between us. He explained that I shouldn't hit females and sent my aunt somewhere, anywhere to calm down. My grands asked me was I okay, I replied yes and he asked me did I know why my aunt attacked me. I explained in another lie, that she was mad that my cousin and I were going to this party and that we didn't invite her. He said to me that she can be silly and demanding all at the same time. I left that day limping outside and met my cousin before he approached the house. He already knew what had happened but he didn't know that I was instead attacked because I wouldn't go through with it.

I made it a point to not visit my grands or if I did, not to stay long. My cousin, I was so happy for him, his family got the opportunity to move into an apartment far enough away from my grands that he too had no reason to visit like I did. Our fun times had just begun; we remained tight and still tight to this day. My road-dog, the brother I never had.

I awoke briefly, my dream ran parallel to the storyline on the TV. I sat up to gather myself and thought about what my aunt had told me that day…she was right. We would be connected for life, but even with our connection, I had a choice to determine how we would stay connected. But I dared not to venture where she took me in our endeavors. Instead I reasoned with myself as to if I've done **it** in any way to someone or have I passed on this behavior through my genes? At that moment I realized that there were now three people that knew my secret including me. Now I had to see firsthand the development of my son looking for ways to expand upon his newly found disease. He was part of my gene pool. My daughters are another handful since they knew before him. They had the capacity to evolve without anyone noticing. They could hold a prison in check, much like me, maybe better. But right now, at this very moment I will go back to sleep and deal with this matter another day.

How do put into words the way I feel?

Life itself has not had the same enlightenment or appeal.

Our day, that day, changed how I viewed what was precious.

You had to subject me to what you thought was best for me? No, best for us?

Since that moment I have borne so much guilt, shame and hate for you.

So once again, I ask you, " Now what am I suppose to do?"

It's about time you come forward to explain your side of our little ordeal.

What you can't? Why? Is it because what I'm saying isn't real?

I want to make you pay for what you did to me, somehow, some way.

But alas I now have to face my own borne demon that I've given away this day...to my kids.

L. Bronson